THE WINYARD FORTUNE

Judith Saxton

G.K. Hall & Co. • **Chivers Press**
Thorndike, Maine USA **Bath, England**

This Large Print edition is published by G.K. Hall & Co., USA and by Chivers Press, England.

Published in 1999 in the U.S. by arrangement with Chivers Press Ltd.

Published in 1999 in the U.K. by arrangement with Severn House Publishers Ltd.

U.S.	Hardcover	0-7838-8566-0	(Romance Series Edition)
U.K.	Hardcover	0-7540-3755-X	(Chivers Large Print)
U.K.	Softcover	0-7540-3756-8	(Camden Large Print)

The text of this Large Print edition is unabridged.
Other aspects of the book may vary from the original edition.

Set in 16 pt. Plantin by Al Chase.

Printed in the United States on permanent paper.

British Library Cataloguing in Publication Data available

Library of Congress Cataloging in Publication Data

Saxton, Judith, 1936–
    The Winyard fortune / Judith Saxton.   673474
      p.   cm.
    "Originally published 1981 under the title Sherida and pseudonym Judy Turner" — T.p. verso.
    ISBN 0-7838-8566-0 (lg. print : hc : alk. paper)
    1. Large type books. 1. Title.
[PR6069.A97W56   1999]
823'.914—dc21
    99-18680

For Julie Redfern,
who enjoyed the rough draft,
and I hope will enjoy the finished
product even more!

CHAPTER ONE

'Well, my dear, the lawyer has arrived. Shall we go down together to hear your mamma's will read, eh?'

Sherida Winyard turned from her contemplation of the steadily falling rain outside the window. Her figure was garbed in deep mourning, but the face which she turned to her stepfather was disconcertingly cheerful.

'Very well, Lord Craven. Let's see if we are to receive our just deserts! Indeed, you are more deserving than I, for I don't mind sick-nursing, whereas you felt yourself to be rather *de trop.*'

Lord Craven, Sherida's third stepfather, said, 'You tended your mamma most faithfully, Sherida. She had little cause to expect such devotion, for I know you saw her seldom.'

Sherida placed her hand on his arm, looking up into his dissipated but good-natured countenance. 'True. And whilst we're being truthful, can I admit I'm not looking forward to the will-reading? I'm sure you'd hate to be my guardian as much as . . .'

'As much as you'd hate to be my ward, eh? Never fear, your mamma knew such an arrangement would be most unsuitable. You've aunts in plenty, however, and . . . Now for it!'

They had crossed the hall while they talked and Lord Craven opened the library door and bowed Sherida through. She smiled at him, taking her place in the chair which old Mr Jobson, the family lawyer, was holding for her. The family, who had gathered for the funeral and stayed over for the will-reading, greeted Sherida according to their natures. Her aunts, Natalie and Bertha, gave her sad half-smiles, her uncles nodded, Great-Uncle Paul Winyard grunted. Only her cousin Bertram grinned and that was because, having lived next door to Knighton all his life, he knew that Sherida and her mamma had been little more than strangers.

Mr Jobson cleared his throat, an expectant hush reigned, and the will-reading began.

Lady Craven, through a series of advantageous marriages, had left a great many possessions, but Sherida listened with little interest whilst various bequests were detailed. Lord Craven was to receive a large sum of money and a property in Yorkshire which Lady Craven had despised as being too far from London; her aunts were left keepsakes and jewellery, small items went to personal friends, mourning rings and sums of money to faithful servants. And then, at last, her own name.

'And to my Daughter, Sherida, I leave in trust all my personal fortune and this manor of Knighton with all its farms and messuages, the said trust to be administered by Lord McNaughton of Albemarle Street, London, until my daughter marries or reaches the age of twenty-five, whichever be the sooner. Such a marriage must be considered suitable by Lord McNaughton and by Lady McNaughton, in whom I place every dependence. It is my wish that my Daughter shall take up residence with the said McNaughtons until the celebration of her marriage, or until she reaches the age of twenty-five, when the estate shall be hers absolutely as previously stated.'

As the lawyer ceased reading a buzz of conversation broke out, and Sherida racked her brains for some recollection of the name McNaughton. Had her mother ever mentioned them? If so, she did not recall it. But Aunt Bertha broke out plaintively, 'The McNaughtons? Why, they're not even *connections!* I really don't see why my dear niece should be sent to strangers. It would be more natural, surely, for her to make her home with Frederick and myself?'

'Letty wasn't a natural parent,' aunt Natalie said spitefully. 'I doubt if she saw Sherida more than half-a-dozen times these past ten years, and being so fond of London life herself, no doubt she felt her daughter, too, would prefer it.'

There was a difficult silence, and then Mr Jobson said, 'Your mother left you a letter, Miss Winyard, to be read when you had heard the will. Would you care to take it into the study and read it alone?'

Sherida took the envelope with a murmured word of thanks and left the room. In the study, sitting comfortably before the fire, she opened it with feelings of lively curiosity. As Aunt Natalie had said, her mother had been almost a stranger to her only daughter until illness had driven her back to Knighton Manor. She had lived for only twelve weeks, growing steadily weaker and more wasted, and when she died Sherida's chief feeling had been one of relief that the other's suffering was at an end.

'You will wonder why I don't leave you in Aunt Bertha's charge, or even with Natalie,' the letter began abruptly. 'The truth is, Natalie knows nothing of the young, being a spinster and set in her ways, and Bertha has her eye on you for her son; he is a poor bargain and I should like you to meet other men. Bertha would scarcely take you to London for a season if she thought she might lose you by so doing! However, my old friend Fanny McNaughton is childless, and I have already ascertained that she will gladly introduce you into society. Lord McNaughton is elderly and something of a philanthropist, and will administer your fortune and estate. You will not be a charge upon their household, for I've made financial arrangements with Jobson, and Lord McNaughton will pay you an allowance out of the estate. Enjoy your first London season, my child, and don't think of wearing mourning. You scarcely knew me, after all! Your Mamma.'

And then, scrawled weakly at the bottom of the page, 'I shall be surprised if you do not "take", as they say, for despite my dislike of being *anyone's* mother, I have found you a delightful companion.'

For an instant, Sherida remembered her mother as she had been in health. Tall, slender and golden-haired, with graceful movements and great, sherry-coloured eyes, the only feature she had passed on to her daughter. So Lady Craven had felt some fondness for her, then, before the end.

Carefully folding the letter and slipping it into her reticule, Sherida felt tears in her eyes. So it had been motherhood, and not her daughter, which Lady Craven had disliked! But it was no use grieving over what could not be helped. She blinked the tears away and returned to the library, where the funeral party was gathering round a cold collation provided by the housekeeper.

'My mother seems to have arranged for me to go to Albemarle Street,' she said quietly to the lawyer. 'I don't know how soon I shall leave here, or . . .'

The old man smiled at her paternally, patting her hand. 'My dear Miss Winyard, your guardian himself has arrived, to carry you back to London with him! I wrote at once, naturally, to acquaint him with your Mamma's sad passing, and he must have set out within hours of receiving my letter. Will you go to him? He's in the crimson salon, and I've instructed your butler to take a tray of luncheon to him presently, for he said he would not intrude upon a family party.'

'Of course,' Sherida said warmly. 'How very good of the old gentleman to come so far! But I suppose he wants to see the estate, talk to the bailiff and so on, if he's to administer it on my behalf.'

And Sherida, determined to show her gratitude as speedily as possible, left the library, crossed the hall, and opened the door of the crimson salon.

For a moment Sherida stopped in the doorway, rivetted by what she saw. Standing in the middle of the hearthrug, glancing towards her with raised brows, was a tall, broad-shouldered man in his thirties. He had thick, dark hair cut in a fashionable brutus and was elegantly clad in a many-caped driving coat which was opened to reveal a glimpse of a blue coat, snowy neckcloth, well-cut breeches and gleaming hessian boots. But what struck her most forcibly after his youth, was the scar which ran across his cheekbone from the corner of his left eye. It gave him a cynical look, and she found she was raising her hand instinctively to her own cheek and hastily lowered it again, feeling her colour rise.

'Miss Winyard?' The man's voice sounded surprised.

'Yes, I'm Sherida Winyard. And you must be . . . Lord McNaughton?' Despite herself she could not help a note of incredulity creeping into her voice.

He bowed, acknowledging it. 'Greville McNaughton. My mother was unable to leave Albemarle Street, but she asked me to be her proxy and to accompany you and your maid back to London as soon as possible. Since I'm to administer your estate, it seemed best that I should come into Norfolk myself.'

'Your . . . Your *Mamma?* But my mother said . . . she thought . . .'

He said a shade impatiently, 'I gather that your mamma didn't realise that my father was a widower with a son of two when he married my step-mamma. But I didn't realise Lady Craven had a daughter, either, until I found myself called upon to become your guardian.'

'Oh. I beg your pardon,' Sherida said. She crossed the room and tugged at the bell-pull, then returned to stand watching him while he shrugged himself out of his coat. 'And your father, sir?'

'Dead, these six years,' he said briefly. The door opened and Simmonds, the butler, majestically took the coat and beaver hat which Lord McNaughton held out, informed them that a tray of luncheon would arrive in a few moments, and quitted the room again.

'Six *years?* And she did not know you, though you both moved in the same circles? Then how . . . ?'

'If you would sit down, Miss Winyard, then I might follow suit,' Lord McNaughton said mildly. After they were seated he continued, 'I was with the army until my father's death, and though I did know Lady Craven, I doubt she knew my name. It seems that she missed the announcement of my father's death, and upon hearing of Lord McNaughton, jumped to the conclusion that he had recovered from his last illness, instead of dying of it! And since we were both christened Greville . . .'

'I *see*, but how dreadful it is,' Sherida said distractedly. 'Then it is you who will manage my affairs! Why did you agree to it?'

'I did not,' he returned, frowning down at his boots. 'My mother did, however. And to do her justice, she had no idea that your mother was dying. She thought it strange, she said, that Letty should begin to talk of her responsibility to you, but she is very good-natured, and . . .'

'Is there no way we can escape from it?' Sherida asked. 'I can't like the arrangement!'

'You can't dislike it more than I, Miss Winyard! But I'll not cheat you, you may be sure of that, and my mother will take good care of you.'

'Cheat me? Oh no, no,' she disclaimed, her colour rising. 'But it must be inconvenient . . . cause you trouble . . .'

He raised one brow. 'Do you intend to be a difficult charge, then, Miss Winyard?'

Her confusion increased, as she was sure he intended. 'Of course not! And I'll do my utmost to see that your guardianship won't last too long!'

He raised both brows at that. 'So you intend to find yourself a husband without loss of time? You're honest, at any rate! But don't forget, your choice must meet with my approval until you're twenty-five. I suppose I could refuse my consent!'

This thought seemed to amuse him, but Sherida jumped to her feet, her cheeks hot. 'Fiddlesticks! You know very well that my mamma intended Lady McNaughton to look after me, with the help of your father. She didn't even know you existed! I'll obey your mamma of course, but you shan't bully me!'

Lord McNaughton had risen when she did and now they stood facing one another across the hearthrug. 'My mother is both easy-going and amenable, Miss Winyard. I'm not going to allow anyone to impose upon her.'

'Then wouldn't it be better if we could change things? Can you not tell my aunt that you'd prefer me to be put in her charge?'

He looked down at her for a moment, his face expressionless. Then he said curtly, 'No, impossible. I tell you my mother agreed eagerly to the conditions! I fear you and I must make the best of it, Miss Winyard.'

Sherida frowned, then her face cleared and she smiled up at him, her eyes dancing. 'How foolish I'm being, my lord, and how ungracious! I do apologise, but this has been a shock for me too, you know. I'll do my best to marry someone of whom you thoroughly approve.

There! How does that sound?'

He could not help laughing and she thought that when he did so, one quite forgot the harsh features and the scarred cheek, and saw that he was a handsome man.

'It sounds generous, Miss Winyard! In my turn, I promise not to bully you, and to do my best to see that you enjoy your come-out.' A knock on the door heralded the entrance of a servant, carrying a laden tray. 'Ah, luncheon! Will you eat with me, or must you return to your relatives in the library?'

As she dressed for dinner, Sherida pondered on Lord McNaughton's attitude. Why has he said he would not have his mother 'imposed on'? Surely he did not mean to imply that she would take advantage of her hostess's kindness? And why should he care whom she married? Obviously, while under his guardianship it would not do for her to encourage the attentions of gazetted fortune-hunters, but the sooner she married, the sooner he would be rid of her! And then, as she put the finishing touches to her appearance, she had her answer.

Aunt Bertha, her husband Frederick and Aunt Natalie had consented to dine with her and had met Lord McNaughton during the afternoon. As she leaned near the mirror to fasten the black velvet ribbon round her throat, she heard voices rising from the terrace below her window. The rain had stopped, to be succeeded by a fine, warm evening, and Aunt Bertha and Aunt Natalie were strolling outside and talking, oblivious of her nearness.

'Of course the reason she's been left in McNaughton's care is obvious, once you've laid eyes on the young man,' Aunt Natalie said clearly. 'Letty was ambitious for the girl, Bertha! I imagine that Fanny McNaughton must have persuaded Letty to give the child into their guardianship for a year or so, and no doubt Letty leapt at the chance. If she doesn't marry young McNaughton I shall be *most* surprised!'

'Sherida may be an heiress, but she's not the finest catch on the marriage market,' Aunt Bertha said plaintively. 'Now if she were to marry my dear Bertram, combining the estates, that would be different.'

'An excellent match for your son, my dear!' Aunt Natalie said with an artificial laugh. 'Not only is the girl worth twice what Bertram will be, but she owns some of the finest agricultural land in the county. Properly administered, her fortune could be trebled before she comes of age. And why should this McNaughton person work to make some other man rich? No, no, you mark my words, it is *he* who will own Knighton, not Bertram!'

'But what good would the land be to him?' Aunt Bertha queried hopefully. 'His estates are in Surrey!'

'Now they are, yes. But didn't you know he's Lord Crome's heir? And his lands . . .'

'March with ours, and consequently, with Knighton. Yes, Natalie, you must be right. Poor Bertram will be heartbroken — I'm sure he considers he and his cousin are as good as betrothed. But there, she may not take McNaughton, for all his title and fortune! I think it might be as well to hire a house in London for the season. I'll speak to Frederick about it.'

The voices died away as the two ladies turned from the terrace to re-enter the house, and Sherida was left to ponder over what she had heard.

Lord McNaughton, busy with the tying of a complicated knot in his wide muslin neckcloth, had no doubts as to why Lady Craven had placed her daughter in his charge. He had driven down to Norfolk seething with annoyance, determined to deny any responsibility for the girl, but the wind had been taken out of his sails the minute he had set eyes on Sherida.

For despite his reassurances to the daughter that his guardianship had been the result of a misunderstanding, he had, in truth, believed that Lady Craven was throwing her child at his head. One glance, however, at his ward's small, heart-shaped face had forced him to admit that she, at any rate, was innocent of any such intention. He had expected to meet a younger edition of Lady Letty; blonde, seductive, self-assured. Instead, Sherida Winyard was small and lively, with chestnut hair and sherry-coloured eyes, clear skin, and a certain wide-eyed innocence which he was sure could not be assumed.

He speedily realised that his mother's hints were true; Lady Letty had had little hand in her daughter's upbringing. Equally obvious, Sherida knew nothing of her mother's behaviour and reputation. Lady Letty had been as free with her favours as any *demi-mondaine*, despite her birth. He disliked her more, perhaps, because in his own salad-days he had been captivated by her for a short time, until he had realised she smiled upon quite half-a-dozen young men as she had smiled upon him. Then, disgusted, Lord McNaughton had ceased to form one of her court.

But when he set eyes on Miss Winyard, he realised it would not be fair to visit his dislike of the mother upon the daughter. She had been badly treated enough already, by all accounts. And if he did not agree to the guardianship, what would happen? She would remain cooped up in the country until she agreed to marry her dull young cousin, or some bluff country squire.

He stood up, shaking down his cuffs. He would play fair by the girl and see that her inheritance throve. He would try to see that she found a good husband and not some ne'er-do-well who would give her a baby every twelvemonth, and then leave her alone on her estate to cope with her growing family whilst he frittered her money away on selfish pleasures.

Resolving, therefore, to fulfil his obligations,

he made his way downstairs feeling righteous. Yes, he would find the child a respectable husband. But it would not be he! Bad blood was bad blood, and Letty Craven had been no better than she should be; he wouldn't tie himself up with her daughter if she were heir to the Golden Ball himself!

CHAPTER TWO

'My darling boy! So here is my ward at last! Why, Sherida, you aren't a bit like your mamma, but your papa had just that twinkling look, and your colouring too. Welcome to Albemarle Street, dear child! Nothing could give me greater pleasure than to have you under my roof!'

Lady McNaughton swooped upon Sherida and enfolded her in a scented embrace, then held her at arms' length the better to examine her.

'I can't pretend I remember you, for you were such a tot, and I don't suppose you remember *me!* I played with you and held you on my knee once, when you were no more than three or four, such a darling little fatty you were!'

'Aunt Fanny!' Sherida exclaimed. 'I could not forget you, for you were so sweet and pretty. And you've not changed one bit!'

Lady McNaughton beamed at her. She was a pretty, lively blonde with big, light blue eyes and a fashionable cupid's-bow mouth. When Sherida dropped her eyes to her hostess's attire, however, she suffered a slight shock. Lady McNaughton was in her late forties, yet she wore a diaphanous robe of blue gauze over a silk slip which clung to her like a second skin. At first glance, indeed, she might have been a girl in her twenties, though a second look showed that her gown had been cut to enhance her best points and her make-up applied to hide her worst ones!

'Mamma, are you going to keep Miss Winyard standing in the hall all afternoon? Why don't you take her to the small salon and ring for some tea? I'm sure Miss Winyard must be thirsty, even if you are not!'

Lady McNaughton laughed and patted her son's cheek. 'Poor darling Greville, how it must annoy you to have a mother so light-minded! Now, Sherida my dear, you must call me Aunt Fanny once again and we must be friends, for I don't feel one *day* older than yourself!'

With an exasperated sigh her son caught hold of her arm, steered her across the hall and through a doorway into an elegant little room, charmingly furnished, with a bright fire burning on the hearth. Crossing the carpet in a couple of strides, he pulled the bell and then turned and smiled affectionately at his parent.

'Now, dear Mamma, all you have to do when Bates comes is to order tea!' He turned to Sherida. 'As you can see, my mamma is not of a practical turn of mind, Miss Winyard!'

'Greville darling, why should I bore myself with practicalities when you seem to *enjoy* ministering to me? And you must call our guest Sherida, not Miss Winyard. So cold, when you're her guardian, dear.' She turned to her guest. 'And you must call my son Greville, of course,' she added kindly.

Sherida noticed with an inward smile the

pained expression which crossed her host's face at this ingenuous suggestion, and waited for him to refute it, but he only said in a bored tone, 'Certainly, Mamma. And now, Miss Winyard, I'll leave you to get to know each other. Tea will be along presently, I feel sure.'

As her hostess chattered on, ordering Bates, when he appeared, to bring macaroons and orange-flavoured sponge cakes as well as tea, Sherida had time to reflect that charming though Lady McNaughton was, she must be quite a trial to her son. No wonder he had not viewed the intrusion into his life of another female with complacence! For it was easy to see that Lady McNaughton would do little for her young guest other than enjoy her company. It would be left to Lord McNaughton to manage her financial affairs and see that she appeared in the right places at the right time.

Lady McNaughton, pouring tea, was blissfully unaware of her guest's silent criticism. 'Our first task,' she declared, handing Sherida a cup, 'must be to refurbish your wardrobe. I'm sure Letty kept you well provided with gowns, but they won't be the sort of garments you'll need for the season.'

'But I'm still in mourning, Aunt Fanny. Would it not seem strange if I bought coloured gowns, and accepted invitations?'

Her hostess's face lightened. 'Mourning! Of course! You've relieved my worst fears, for I could not *think* why a girl with your colouring should be wearing black, unless you had bad taste, which I was sure could not be the case, for dear Letty always knew *precisely* what suited her! And your mamma wrote me that she would not hear of you wearing mourning, so her wishes must weigh with us above all else!'

'I do feel morbid and guilt-ridden in black, knowing that I cannot feel as sad as I ought,' Sherida confessed. 'But ball dresses, Aunt Fanny? Surely I should not dance? What will people think?'

'Oh, pooh, London people aren't so narrow-minded,' Lady McNaughton said grandly, rather spoiling the effect by adding ingenuously, 'And anyway, you're an heiress, dearest, which will make your behaviour acceptable to the most strait-laced! But I see you've finished your tea, so let's go to your room and examine the clothes you've brought with you. I do trust not *all* black?'

'No, but they're all dull,' Sherida admitted.

They had crossed the hall and were ascending the stairs, when Lord McNaughton came running down the flight towards them.

'We're just going to Sherida's room, Greville, to see what new clothes she will need,' Lady McNaughton told her son. 'I expect we shall spend *days* shopping, for you will want your ward to be a credit to us both!'

'If you think it right, Lord McNaughton,' Sherida began anxiously, 'for me . . .'

He cut her short, his voice chilly with reproof.

24

'My mother can certainly be trusted on this score, Miss Winyard, and no one could better assist you in choosing suitable garments with which to dazzle the *ton!* As her guest, she will see you do as you ought. But since I am your banker, I beg you not to spend too freely!'

She shrank back a little, saying in a subdued voice, 'I'm sorry, I didn't mean . . . that is, I intended no criticism . . .' She caught the apologetic tone in her voice and scowled, forcing herself to add, 'Though how can I keep within the limits of my allowance when I don't know how much it is to be? Perhaps before you censure the possibility of my over-spending you might acquaint me with the sum at my disposal!'

He gave her a glinting look, then a grin. 'So the kitten has claws, eh? Very good, Miss Winyard, I'll pay your bills out of the money which your lawyer has placed at my disposal and then I'll work out a quarterly allowance, so that you may know the sum at your command and may not outrun the constable! So you see, your financial affairs, at least, are in safe hands!'

He patted her shoulder and before she could answer he was continuing down the stairs and Lady McNaughton, now standing on the landing above, called as though there had been no break in their conversation, 'Muslins are useful, and Indian cotton is popular, and you'll want . . .'

Chattering gaily, she led her charge into the room which had been set aside for her.

25

Having found Sherida's entire wardrobe un-suitable, the the next few days passed in a whirl of shopping but at last Lady McNaughton pro-nounced herself satisfied.

'The invitations to your ball, which will launch you into society, have been sent, of course,' she told Sherida impressively. 'I don't think I've for-gotten anyone of consequence, but we must not forget you've relatives in Town. Did you ever hear of your Aunt Caroline?'

'Aunt Caroline? Was she my Papa's sister?'

'Yes, she was. Is, I should say. She lives in London you know, because she had to sell a lot of the Tilney property when she was widowed. And she has a son, Roland, who is of an age with Greville, and a daughter, Diane, who's just eigh-teen. Naturally, I'm invited them, but I thought it might be a little difficult for you to meet quite *close* relatives for the first time at your coming-out dance. So if you don't object, I'll ask them to dine tomorrow night.'

'That would be lovely. I know so few people, Aunt Fanny, that even the dullest cousins would be acceptable.'

'I wouldn't describe them as *dull,* exactly,' lady McNaughton said reflectively. 'Roland, indeed, is far from dull, and Caroline is a most determined woman. I can't speak of your cousin Diane, for she's not yet out, so I've not met her. But we'll remedy that tomorrow night.'

The two women were sitting in the small

salon, comfortable sandals on their feet, their shopping done for the day, and when Lord McNaughton walked into the room their exhausted attitudes made him smile.

'You look worn to a thread, Mamma,' he said, lifting his mother's hand and lightly kissing the palm. 'But I suppose you enjoy your exertions, or you could send Miss Winyard out with a maid for chaperon.' He turned to Sherida. 'And even you look less animated than usual. I do trust the pile of boxes in the hall is the end, at last, of this orgy of buying?'

Unable to convince herself that she was not wickedly overspending, Sherida blushed hotly, but before she could reply Lady McNaughton cried, 'Fie on you, Greville! What else should we do but shop, with Sherida's first ball less than ten days away? And dearest, you remember the Tilneys? I've invited them to dine with us to-morrow night, to meet Sherida, and . . .'

He had been leaning against the mantel, smiling down at them with an expression of gentle mockery, but at this he stood upright, frowning intently down upon his mother. 'Sir Roland Tilney? Dining here? What on earth . . .'

Lady McNaughton cut in, hands fluttering in warning. 'Greville, dearest! Caroline Tilney was Richard Winyard's eldest sister, and is thus Sherida's aunt. We could scarcely not invite them to the ball, and I thought it best that they should dine and meet Sherida first. Indeed, Roland and his mamma may be met *everywhere*,

27

and since Diane is to make her come-out this year too, it would be nice for Sherida to become friendly with her.'

Lord McNaughton frowned. 'You don't have to justify your actions to me, Mamma,' he said with obvious untruthfulness. 'It is none of my concern who you invite to this ball. And as you say, the Tilneys are to be met everywhere.' He turned and strolled out of the room, leaving the two women gazing silently after him.

'Oh, dear,' Lady McNaughton said as the door closed behind her son. 'I forgot that . . . Well, Greville can be a trifle . . . But he and Roland meet with perfect amity at their clubs and Almack's, and I thought . . . However, we shall go ahead with our plans.'

'Indeed, ma'am, I don't in the least mind meeting the Tilneys for the first time at the ball, if it would ease matters,' Sherida said, trying not to show the curiosity which was consuming her. She paused delicately. 'Is there something about my cousin Roland that I should know, perhaps? Is he a *rake?*'

'A rake? I wouldn't say that. I don't scruple to tell you, dearest, that Greville and he have probably quarrelled. Greville's manner has caused him to quarrel with a great many people at one time or another. If I were only to invite my son's close friends to the house, it would be very thin of company indeed!'

On the evening that the Tilneys were to dine,

Sherida descended the stairs in a primrose gown with a gauze overdress in a deeper yellow, feeling considerable trepidation. But Lord McNaughton, ushering her into the room where they would receive their guests, dispelled her nervousness by making her cross instead.

'You look charming, but you really must not look so frightened,' he said as they heard the butler escorting their guests across the hall. 'Come now, smile and hold your head up!'

Shooting him a look of fury, Sherida glided across the room in Lady McNaughton's wake, head high, back straight — and made an instant impression on one member of the party. Aunt Caroline was small and dumpy, with a determined jaw and a fixed smile; Diane a tall brunette with a full figure; but it was Cousin Roland who brought the colour flaming to Sherida's cheeks. He was taller than his sister and even darker, with a wing of black hair falling romantically — and intentionally — across his broad white brow. Dark brown eyes fringed with long black lashes fixed themselves on Sherida's small face with unsmiling intensity, and his gaze never left her for a moment while Lady McNaughton performed the introductions.

When at last he shook her hand it was a relief to smile naturally, able to acknowledge his burning glance and to say how much she was enjoying her stay in London, and how nice it was to meet her cousins.

'I'm glad. For you are very different from your

mamma,' he said, taking her hand and holding it in his own. 'Cousin Sherida, I hope we shall be . . . good friends! Are you able to ride with me? Drive in the park?'

Lady McNaughton, who had apparently been deep in conversation with Lady Tilney, said lightly, over her shoulder, 'Don't press her to accept invitations yet, Roland dear. It would not be at all the thing until after the ball which is to introduce her. Once that is over, *then* she may drive with you, and walk with you,' an infinitesimal pause, 'if she wishes to do so.'

'But cousins should be friends,' Diane said warmly. 'You may walk with *me*, may she not, Lady McNaughton, before her ball? And then I can introduce my cousin to other girls who make their come-out this season.'

Before Lady McNaughton could reply the butler came quietly into the room and caught his lordship's eye. In the bustle of the two younger men politely giving an arm to the older ladies, and Sherida and Diane laughingly clasping hands, no answer was given, but Sherida thought that it might be fun to walk with Diane, and very much hoped that Lady McNaughton's consent would be forthcoming.

During the meal Roland behaved well and did not again stare so embarrassingly at Sherida, instead giving his attention to his mother and Lady McNaughton, chatting charmingly to them both and drawing Lord McNaughton into the conversation so that the two girls began to become quietly acquainted.

After they had left the men to their port, Lady McNaughton announced her intention of taking Lady Tilney up to her room for a chat, and advised Sherida and Diane to talk likewise. Sherida was anxious to get to know her cousin better, so the two girls climbed the stairs and entered Sherida's pretty bedchamber.

'Cousin, I must apologise for the way my brother stared,' Diane said as soon as the door shut behind them. 'I could see he was very struck by you, but he should have remembered it is ill-bred to fix one's gaze so.'

'I thought I must have a smut on my nose,' Sherida responded frankly, picking up her brush and attacking her soft curls. 'But then I'm not used to parties, and I'd best become used to being stared at, for though I know I'm not anything out of the ordinary, I'm Letty Craven's daughter, and an object of curiosity to those who never even knew she had a child!'

'Indeed, you're very pretty,' Diane said earnestly. 'But I'm glad Roland didn't offend you. And another thing, dear Sherida, we would so much like to offer you our hospitality this season, especially as you and I are both coming out together. If you would explain to Lord McNaughton that you would rather that the *family* undertook the task of bringing you into society, I'm sure we could persuade him to let you come to us. My mamma charged me to suggest it to you, should the opportunity arise.'

'That's impossible.' Sherida said firmly. 'I'm the McNaughtons' ward, you know, and could not even suggest such a thing.' She was rather surprised to find that she had not the slightest desire to move in with her aunt and cousins, however pleasant they might seem, but was careful not to let a trace of her feelings show in her voice or expression.

'I feared as much,' Diane agreed sadly. 'It would have been so lovely to have you staying with us, but in the circumstances . . .'

She left the sentence unfinished and Sherida, her hair tidied, said, 'Shall we join the others?' and moved towards the door.

'One moment,' Diane said, catching her arm. 'Lord McNaughton is an attractive man, is he not? Perhaps more attractive for his scarred cheek, we foolish females might think! But as you may have guessed, he's not reached the age of thirty-two without having his fair share of . . . experiences. So while you live under his roof, it might be as well to make it clear that you are by no means living in his pocket!'

'Dianne, how can you be so ignorant when you've lived in London for years?' Sherida asked incredulously. 'Even I know better than to live in any man's pocket!'

She moved towards the door again but once more, Diane detained her. 'My dear cousin, don't think I thought you such a goose. But you may be coerced into accepting Lord McNaughton's escort simply because you're living beneath his roof, and I just wanted you to know that if you need squiring to a party or picnic, my brother . . .'

'Lord McNaughton hasn't shown the slightest desire to squire me anywhere,' Sherida said. 'Are you trying to suggest he has an interest in me other than his duties as my guardian?'

Diane was beginning to look harassed. 'No, no, cousin. It's just that . . . well, if his attentions do begin to seem too particular . . .'

Sherida faced her squarely, a challenge in her eyes. 'Why should he pay me particular attention? He's rich enough not to be interested in *my* inheritance! And he's Crome's heir, I understand, so far from being on the catch for an heiress, heiresses must be on the catch for him!'

'Yes. But Crome's land marches with Knighton,' Diane said with the air of one telling an unpleasant truth. 'There, I've said the worst, and if you're angry with me I have only myself to blame. But I didn't know if you were aware of all the facts. Lord McNaughton usually dances attendance upon very sophisticated females, and if he does pay you any attention — well, Knighton would round off the Crome estates very nicely, should we say!'

'We should say nothing of the sort,' Sherida retorted firmly. 'Gossip can be dangerous, Diane. As for your brother, I'm much obliged to him for his offer to squire me to parties, but though he's my cousin, I know less of him, if anything, than I do of Lord McNaughton. And since he and my guardian are much the same age, I suppose Sir Roland, too, has had his fair share of . . . experiences!'

This carrying of the war into the enemies' camp was something which plainly discomfited Diane. She blushed and lowered her eyes, saying evasively, 'Roland is not *inexperienced,* precisely, but the cases are not at all similar. However, let's not quarrel! It was wrong of me to interfere, though I did so with the best intentions. Do forgive me, and then we may be friends!'

She spoke with such sincerity that Sherida's heart melted, and she caught her cousin's hand impulsively in her own. 'Diane, you are the first friend of my own age I've ever had, and I fall out with you! Don't take offence because I can't take your warnings seriously, but the McNaughtons have been so kind. I cannot hear doubts cast on their goodness, can I?'

'No, of course not,' Diane said, embracing the smaller girl warmly. 'And I'm being a goose, raising alarms for which there is probably no need. Shall we arrange to meet in the morning, for a walk in the park?'

'That would be delightful,' Sherida concurred. 'Where shall we meet?'

Diane said that she would come to Albemarle Street, and then they could walk in the park if the weather was fine and talk indoors if it was not.

'And I won't suggest that Roland might walk with us, for after all, it is only a few days to your

34

ball, after which we shall both be counted as truly "out", and may meet friends and suitors without censure when we're walking,' she said merrily, and she and Sherida descended into the hall, the best of friends once more.

CHAPTER THREE

The night of the ball in Albemarle Street came at last. Sherida had walked in the park with Diane several times, had a nodding acquaintance with several of her cousin's girl friends, and had received interested glances from a number of young men. But tonight, in her loveliest evening dress, she would be brought into society proper, under Lady McNaughton's aegis.

When she swept down the staircase in gleaming white satin, with her mother's pearls round her neck and a sheaf of dark yellow rose-buds in the crook of her arm, she knew she was looking her best. At the foot of the stairs, Lord McNaughton watched her descent, a little smile hovering at the corners of his mouth, his scarred cheek looking rakish and interesting above the sombre splendours of his evening dress.

'Very nice, Miss Winyard,' he commented. 'I like your hair dressed high; it's a style which becomes a small female, though it tends to make tall girls look enormous.'

But this disappointing response to her splendid appearance was not repeated when their first guests arrived. The Tilneys, in honour of their relationship to Sherida, were to dine with the family first, and Sir Roland, kissing her hand reverently, did so with the air of one almost blinded by her beauty. Though his stammered

36

comment that she looked 'the prettiest thing I've seen' might have been somewhat fulsome, it was pleasant to be courted and praised. Much pleasanter, Sherida told herself firmly, than to be told condescendingly that one looked 'very nice', which remark was followed in the same breath by a reminder that she was only a little creature, after all!

So, when the dancing at last began, she was in charity with Sir Roland, and somewhat out of it with Lord McNaughton, particularly when she saw him with a thin, brittle-looking blonde whose nervous, excitable laugh and the habit she had of touching her curls every two minutes, as though to assure herself that her head had not fallen off, had already made Sherida think her a poor creature.

Contrary to her expectations, in fact, Lord McNaughton took scarcely any notice of her, apart from that which good manners demanded, and Roland scarcely left her side, except when she was dancing — which was almost cease-lessly.

Her annoyance mounting, she took to the floor with various partners, to see Lord McNaughton either dancing with one of a small group of sophisticated women in their mid-twenties, or chatting to friends. She told herself that the *last* thing she wanted was to dance with him, and that this way at least there would be no ugly rumours flying round that he was trying to fix her interest, but she found herself smiling more and more warmly at Roland, particularly when Lord McNaughton was in their vicinity.

'Your guardian certainly believes in dispensing his favours freely,' he remarked once, indicating Lord McNaughton, who was surrounded by women. 'He finds favour with Sally Jersey and Caroline Lamb, and even the Princess Esterhazy laughs and jokes with him.'

'He is the host,' Sherida reminded him. 'He has to see to the comfort of all his guests.'

'Yes, no one could accuse him of failing to circulate,' Roland agreed. He smiled down at her. 'Would you like to have some supper now? It is a little early, but . . .'

'Oh not yet,' Sherida protested. 'But where is Di, Roland? I don't want to neglect her!'

'I think she's on the terrace, with the young Willoughby lad,' Sir Roland said. 'Shall I escort you to her?'

'Oh! Is it all right to go to the terrace?' Sherida said doubtfully. 'Very well then, Roland, if we can go at once. I've a partner for the next set.'

They made their way out through the long windows at the far end of the ballroom. It was a fine, moonlight night and the sweet, frail scents of spring rose to their nostrils from the garden as they crossed the paving and went towards the balustrade. There were several groups of people standing about on the terrace, but though Sherida strained her eyes in the fitful moonlight and shadow, she could not see her cousin.

'Surely she has not gone into the garden?'

Roland wondered aloud. He indicated a flight of shallow steps, leading down to the lawn. 'Shall we . . .'

'Sherida!'

Sherida turned with a start, to find Lord McNaughton standing at her elbow.

'What are you doing out here? That dress is too thin for night-wandering.' He turned to Roland. 'Are you searching for your sister, Tilney? I saw her take Miss Upton to one of the bedchambers. The poor creature has torn her flounce, and Miss Tilney is to help her effect repairs. You had best go in search of her, and I will escort Miss Winyard back to my mamma.'

Rather to Sherida's surprise Roland glanced undecidedly down at her, then at his host, and then, muttering something she could not catch, made off indoors, looking remarkably sheepish.

Sherida turned to Lord McNaughton, and put her hand on his arm so that he might lead her indoors. 'But it was I who wanted Diane,' she said reflectively. 'So why did my cousin go back indoors in such a hurry?'

Lord McNaughton smiled; she could see his teeth gleam whitely in the moonlight. Then he turned her gently round, so that they were facing the parapet with their backs to the houselights.

'Roland has gone back indoors in a hurry because he knows he had no right to bring you out on the terrace,' he said. 'I have tried not to interfere with your pleasures, Miss Winyard, but you leave me little choice. Your cousin Roland is *not* a very eligible suitor, you know.'

Sherida said stiffly, 'He is not rich, perhaps, but . . .'

'No, he is not rich. But he is, my dear little innocent, a rake, and known, moreover, to be hanging out for a rich wife. He's not had much luck since he eloped with a little heiress straight out of the schoolroom two or three years ago. Mammas have tended to guard their daughters from his attentions. But you have no mamma to shelter you, which is why I have spoken so frankly.'

'But . . . but I have *your* mamma,' Sherida said, her voice shaking a little.

'You have indeed, and no doubt she will mention the matter to you. But her position is difficult, is it not? He is, in truth, your cousin!'

'Yes, I do see,' Sherida nodded. 'But why did you follow me out here, why did you not let your mother tell me, after the party?'

'Because you are a pretty little creature, and I thought Roland might try to take advantage of your youth and inexperience.'

She tilted her chin and looked up into his eyes, her own sparkling provocatively. 'I thank you, Lord McNaughton, but I am quite capable of taking care of myself!'

'Are you?' he asked softly. She saw him glance round, and then with one swift movement he pulled her into his arms and his lips found hers.

The kiss had been meant to punish her, she felt sure, for her presumption in resenting his authority, but somehow that did not happen. As his arms locked her body close to his she was so shocked that she instinctively raised her hands to push him away. But then a wild warmth tingled through her body, so that her lips softened involuntarily beneath his, and he prolonged the kiss until she was breathless and trembling, her knees weak, though her heart hammered a great pulse from the top of her head to the tips of her toes.

Then, abruptly, he put her away from him, his eyes mocking in the fitful moonlight. 'Take care of yourself? You've no more idea how to repulse a man's advances than . . . than a kitten! Or else there is more of your mother in you than I'd realised. Let that be a lesson to you — don't walk in the moonlight with experienced rakes!'

Sherida's heartbeats were slowing to normal and she felt giddy from the strength of emotions which fought within her. Anger finally won. She said coldly, looking straight up at him, 'I didn't know you were an experienced rake! How am I supposed to tell?'

His teeth gleamed as he smiled, flinging up a hand. '*Touché!* But I didn't mean myself, as you very well know! I had not the slightest intention of seducing you, I only kissed you to prove that you are simply not capable of taking care of yourself! But Roland has few scruples, and I'm very sure that he means business this time. You may not be a great heiress, but you're worth a tidy sum, Miss Winyard, and will be worth more as your land improves.'

He took her arm in a hard grasp, leading her back across the terrace to the ballroom. Lady McNaughton, seeing them, waved, the anxious look on her face being replaced by a smile.

'Your mamma is looking for me, I'd best go to her,' Sherida muttered, still shaken by her recent experience. 'And whatever you may say about my cousin Roland, Lord McNaughton, *he* behaved like a gentleman towards me!'

'Which is more than I did, eh? Well, I won't offend you again. But remember, I shall be watching! I've no desire to find my mother or myself being blamed because you've made a little fool of yourself!'

She winced at the hard note in his voice, but said in a small voice, 'I'll be more careful in future — and *not* just with my cousin, sir!'

He laughed, then moved away from her, back to the group he had left, and Sherida made her way across to Lady McNaughton.

'Sherida, my dear one, you *worried* me,' she said reproachfully as soon as her ward was near enough. 'It will not *do*, you know, to go out on to the terrace with your cousin Roland. Oh, he is a very charming young man, but one has to be careful. I would have sent Greville after you, except that I couldn't find him. How irritating it is that one's children disappear when one needs them!'

'Lord McNaughton was on the terrace,' Sherida assured her bitterly. 'Don't worry, dear Aunt Fanny, your son has made it quite clear that I must not linger on dark terraces with rakish young men!'

But this attempt at sarcasm was lost on Lady McNaughton, who said, with transparent relief, 'Oh, I am *glad,* dearest, because I am *not* good at giving moral lectures, even when I know I ought! Now let us talk of pleasanter things! To whom are you engaged for the supper dance?'

The rest of the evening passed without incident, save that Sherida found herself reluctant to spend too much time in Roland's company. Lord McNaughton's strictures on her cousin's behaviour, whether true or false, had certainly made her aware that Roland's attitude towards her was a little too warm for their short acquaintance. So when Diane suggested meeting next day to talk over their evening, she said firmly that she was sorry, but she and Lady McNaughton would probably have a quiet morning at home, and would be visiting friends in the afternoon.

Diane accepted this, but not without giving her friend a speculative look, and Sherida found herself almost regretting that she had ever met either of her cousins.

When everyone had gone and the servants began to tidy up, the McNaughtons and Sherida took themselves off to the small salon, with hot chocolate and biscuits, to discuss the success of the evening.

'I am delighted with your reception,' Lady McNaughton said as soon as they had settled themselves comfortably before the glowing fire. 'Oh, I expected you to be popular with the young men, dearest, for you are so *very* pretty, but even the older people — people of *my* generation, that is — said how pleasant and unaffected you were. Invitations will pour in for you, mark my words.' She paused, then added carefully, 'And your cousin Diane, though her looks are not above the average, seemed to be enjoying herself. You like her, do you?'

'Yes, she's charming,' Sherida said. 'Very friendly.'

'I see. And how do you find Roland?'

'He seems very nice, Aunt Fanny. He wants to take me driving, and says he will teach me to handle a phaeton and pair. But . . .'

'His attentions were almost suffocatingly obvious, were they not?' Lady McNaughton nodded sympathetically. 'But you'll learn quickly enough how to deal with men who try so desperately to charm! Turn off the compliments with a laugh and a shrug, don't answer questions which attempt to put you on too intimate a footing. I could tell you a hundred ways of damping pretensions without being cruel or obvious, but I daresay you'll know them all soon enough!'

'And what about men who have no charm whatsoever?' Sherida said waspishly, her eyes going involuntarily to the quiet figure of her host, sitting in a chair well back from the fire, so that he was in shadow. 'The ones who don't even have the good manners to . . . to *tell* you things, but are quick enough to give you a dressing-down when you do wrong?'

Before Lady McNaughton could answer, a lazy voice said, 'Don't worry Mamma, that remark was addressed to me — or perhaps I should say fired at me! I'm sorry, Miss Winyard, if my lack of charm offended you on the terrace, but at the time it seemed quite otherwise! You see, Mamma, Miss Winyard thought herself quite capable of keeping Tilney, and others like him, at arm's length, so I . . .'

'Please!' Sherida said sharply, terrified lest he should tell his mother the whole story. 'It was bad enough . . .'

She saw his teeth gleam as he smiled. 'Quite. But you'll be more sensible in future, I feel sure.'

Lady McNaughton looked from one to the other, her eyes bright with curiosity, but she only said, 'Very well then, no more lectures! And now, if you've finished your chocolate, dearest, we ought to make our way to bed, or we shall be wrecks in the morning.'

Sherida obediently got to her feet, but as she moved past Lord McNaughton he rose and caught her arm, holding her back for a moment. 'I want to talk to you in the morning,' he said. 'If you have planned to meet your cousins or any other friends, tell me, and I shall cancel the appointment for you.'

'I've no appointments, but what do you want to talk to me about? You've done your share of

'. . . talking . . . tonight,' Sherida replied stiffly, and saw his mouth curve in a reminiscent smile.

'You said just now that I'd not had the good manners to *tell* you things; tomorrow I shall remedy that. No, no, don't shake your head! I shall take you driving in Kensington Gardens to-morrow after breakfast. Goodnight, Miss Winyard!'

Sherida wondered quite seriously whether to obey Lord McNaughton's peremptory instructions, or whether to lie late in bed, or get up early and go out without him. But neither of these plans seemed feasible. He rose early, she knew that, and very likely he would catch her stealing down the front steps, and give her another lecture on her behaviour. And she had horrid visions of his penetrating her bedchamber and ordering her to get up, if she tried to remain in bed.

So it was in a mood of reluctant defiance that she dressed herself in her elegant almond-green walking dress, her half-boots, and her long, ruched silk gloves, and set off down the stairs. Lady McNaughton was still in bed and Sherida had breakfasted in her own room, so she hesitated at the foot of the stairs, not knowing where she should await Lord McNaughton. But the problem was solved by his coming out of the morning-room with his quick, self-assured stride, and checking to greet her.

'Good morning, Miss Winyard, you're ready

betimes, I see. I've told my groom to bring the horses round to the front door in ten minutes, so you may wait in the salon until then. I have an urgent letter to write.'

She inclined her head but did not answer, and this seemed to annoy him, for his lips tightened, and he said sharply, 'Don't sulk, please. Try to remember I like my role of bear-leader as little as you like yours of protégée!'

He was gone before she could answer, and she walked into the salon trembling with annoyance. Bear-leader, indeed! She had done her best to behave well, and but for accompanying Roland on to the terrace, she thought she had behaved just as she ought. In fact, Lady McNaughton had told her so. And Lord McNaughton had already put her off darkened terraces, she told herself crossly, by *mauling* her as if she were a kitchen-maid, though she was sorry to note that even to her inward ear, her words lacked conviction.

She fell to wondering whether being kissed by Roland would have been as heart-stopping an experience as being kissed by Lord McNaughton had proved to be, and was deep in speculation when the door opened and Lord McNaughton stood before her. Blushing as brightly as though he had read her thoughts, she got to her feet with as much dignity as she could muster, and went before him down the front steps and across to his phaeton.

He helped her up, climbed into the driving

seat, and said to his groom, 'Stand aside from their heads, Boswell! I shall be gone no more than an hour or so.'

For a while he concentrated on his driving, for the road was crowded, but presently he glanced down at her, smiling slightly.

'Well, Miss Winyard! I must apologise for being abrupt with you this morning. The truth is, I had not thought it necessary to lay down rules of conduct for you, supposing that you would know what would be socially acceptable, and thinking my mamma would put you right when you were in doubt. But perhaps it would be wiser to point out the pitfalls, rather than watch you fall into them first! For a start, *never* leave a ballroom with a man alone, no matter how closely related he may be.'

Sherida said, with what good grace she could muster, 'No, I understand now that I did wrong.'

He nodded, accepting the acknowledgement of her fault carelessly. 'And at picnics, break-fasts, etcetera, don't go off with a man by yourself.'

She said with a trace of impatience, 'I've said I won't do so.'

He took his eyes off the road for a moment, sweeping her with an enigmatic glance. 'So you did. And another simple rule for you to follow might be that before you accept any invitations you should consult either my mother or myself. That will ensure you don't get into any bad scrapes, such as going to a public ball unchaperoned, or visiting persons who are not well thought of. You may think I am being unduly censorious, but I assure you, you could easily ruin yourself in the eyes of the more old-fashioned by some such innocent action.'

'I take it that driving alone with a man in a phaeton — providing his name happens to be Lord McNaughton — is perfectly in order?' Sherida enquired blandly. 'But of course, should his name chance to be Tilney, that would be a different matter!'

He grinned down at her, and she could not help smiling back.

'Oh, you may drive with Tilney, if you wish to do so,' he allowed carelessly. 'But I don't think he should teach you to drive. London is not suitable for such activities, and Tilney is not the master of the art he might pretend. Now be a good child, consult either my mamma or myself before you act, and we may yet remain friends.'

'Not forgetting, at the end of the day, that you may object to any friends I happen to make,' Sherida said rebelliously. 'And I am *not* a child!'

'You are certainly not a *good* child,' he countered, flashing another provocative look at her face. 'But if you do as you're told, you may yet attain a place in my regard! Have you been to Kensington Gardens before? This is the main entrance.'

'No, this is my first visit,' Sherida said. 'Oh, how pretty!' They were driving down a walk lined with willow trees, with primroses blooming in the grass. 'I wish I might stroll along here for a little.'

'So you may, if you chance to see an acquaintance with whom I may safely leave you for half-an-hour,' he replied equably. 'Then I will drive back through the gardens and take you up once more. What about Miss Huxtable, the young lady in the pink pelisse there? I believe I saw you talking to her last night, with your cousin.'

'Oh, and Di is with her,' Sherida exclaimed. 'Please, sir, will you put me down for a little?'

He said shortly, 'I did not see Miss Tilney, but you may walk with them, of course. I shall drive round to see your man of business regarding your allowance, and come back here in thirty minutes. Don't leave the gardens.'

'No, of course not,' Sherida promised. 'Thank you for the drive, Lord McNaughton, and for the advice.'

He nodded, drawing the phaeton to a halt and Sherida jumped nimbly down and as he drove off, greeted Diane.

'Darling!' Diane said, kissing her cousin's cheek. 'You remember Miss Huxtable? I thought you were having a quiet morning with Lady McNaughton!'

'Yes, so did I,' Sherida responded gloomily. Miss Huxtable, a round-faced, cheerful young woman, said brightly, 'I *did* enjoy the party, Miss Winyard! And I think your guardian is charming. To be sure, the scar makes him look a little grim, but . . .'

'I'm glad you enjoyed the party,' Sherida said carefully. 'As for Lord McNaughton being charming —' She hesitated, realising belatedly that it did not become her to criticise her host.

Diane, however, had no such scruples. 'My brother said Lord McNaughton censured your behaviour in walking on the terrace with him,' she remarked. 'It was too bad of him, for Roland is your cousin! And besides, you were not precisely alone out there!'

'But the others were in groups,' Sherida felt constrained to point out. 'It *was* foolish of me, Di, for innocent though it was, it could have caused talk.'

'Then the fault was Roland's,' Diane said. 'He thought nothing of it, however, supposing to find me outside with Mr Willoughby.'

'If it was wrong for me to walk on the terrace with your brother, why should it be all right for you to walk there with Mr Willoughby?' Sherida asked in an aggrieved tone. It seemed that there was one set of rules for everyone but herself!

Miss Huxtable, who had been listening to the exchange with interest, intervened to say, 'Oh, Miss Winyard, it would have been every bit as bad! I expect Sir Roland was trying to get his sister out of a scrape, or he would never so far forgotten himself as to have taken you outside!'

Sherida felt relief flooding through her. She should have guessed that someone as thoughtful

51

and charming as her cousin would not have deliberately caused her to offend. His intentions, then, had been completely honourable, which was more than could be said for Lord McNaughton. She smiled brilliantly at Miss Huxtable. 'I wonder what made him think that Diane was on the terrace, though?'

Diane said without hesitation, 'Why, because I *had* been walking there, I'm afraid! Not that there was any harm in it for I was with Miss Upton, her brother Charles, and Mr Willoughby. But apparently when Roland saw me leave the ballroom he thought I was alone with Mr Willoughby. And then he missed my return, when I took Miss Upton to your maid to have her flounce stitched up. I am so sorry, dear Sherida, that you seem to have suffered for it.'

'Oh well, I didn't precisely *suffer*,' Sherida said airily. 'Lord McNaughton merely told me to be more careful, or I should have all the old dowagers gossiping about me.'

Diane began to reassure her when a phaeton drew up alongside and a familiar voice said warmly, 'Cousin Sherida! You naughty little creature, you said you would not be walking out today! But come, now that I've found you, you must give me the pleasure of your company on a drive round the gardens, or I shall take offence, I promise you I shall!'

Sherida looked up into her cousin's darkly handsome face. He was sporting a many-caped driving coat and had a handkerchief knotted round his neck; his curly-brimmed beaver was cocked over his brow at a rakish angle, and his nether regions were resplendently clad in primrose pantaloons.

'Hello, Cousin! I will certainly drive with you, but I must be back here, on this path, in about fifteen minutes, because Lord McNaughton has arranged to return for me. He only set me down for a little while, so that I might talk to your sister.'

She climbed into the phaeton, and her cousin drove at a brisk trot around the gardens, admiring the spring flowers which were breaking into blossom.

'The weather is improving as spring advances,' Sir Roland said presently, when she had exclaimed at the misty beginning of a bluebell patch in a distant thicket. 'It would be pleasant, would it not, to make up a party and visit Vauxhall one evening? I am sure Lady McNaughton would not object.'

'I'm sure she would not, if your mamma would be present? I have no desire to set up people's backs by behaving in a . . . a *fast* fashion!'

'Naturally,' he agreed understandingly. 'None of us are so firmly fixed in society's good graces that we can afford to flout its conventions. And by the same token, I hope Lord McNaughton realised that it was thoughtlessness which led me to walk you on to the terrace in search of Diane? But I imagined that, as we are cousins, nothing would be said.'

'Cousin Roland, I am heartily sick of the sound of the word terrace,' Sherida said. 'Diane has explained, and that is enough for me. And now may we turn back, please, to the path where you took me up? Otherwise I shall really be in Lord McNaughton's black books.'

'Very well, I will turn at the end of this avenue,' he said obligingly. 'Just let me draw to one side for a moment so that this phaeton may pass.'

'Oh, it *is* Lord McNaughton,' said Sherida. 'Thank you for a delightful ride, Roland.'

She climbed down, called her farewell, and climbed into the other phaeton.

'I do hope I'm not late, sir?' she said anxiously to Lord McNaughton, as her cousin waved and drove off. 'I *did* walk with my cousin and Miss Huxtable, and then Sir Roland accosted me, and begged me to ride a short way with him.'

'Which you were happy to do, of course,' he said sardonically.

'Yes, I was,' Sherida returned, stung by his tone. 'And I was glad I did, for I have now heard the true story of last night's walk on the terrace.'

Lord McNaughton raised one brow. 'The *true* story? Have I told you a false one, then?'

'Oh, no, I didn't mean that,' Sherida stammered, momentarily discomposed. If only he were not so quick to take the offensive! 'The fact is, sir, that Roland saw his sister leave the ballroom with Mr Willoughby. He did not realise she was with another couple as well, so thought it best to follow her and persuade her to return to the ballroom. He had no idea that by so doing, he might cause me embarrassment.'

'Dear me! Now what made me think him a knowing one?' murmured Lord McNaughton. 'Quite green, isn't he, to see a danger to his sister yet none to you?'

'Naturally he would be more concerned for his sister than for me,' Sherida said indignantly. 'And he *is* my cousin!'

'As you seem to have told me several times before,' he agreed suavely. 'Why is it, Miss Winyard, that whenever you and I are alone for a few moments the conversation turns on Sir Roland Tilney? I wish it would not, for he is by no means my favourite subject.'

Sherida opened her mouth to speak, stopped, and shot a suspicious look at her companion.

'Don't say you were going to tell me again, that he *is* your cousin?' Lord McNaughton said incredulously, with a slight smile. 'That is positively the only reason I can think of for your silence!'

Sherida tried to frown, failed, and chuckled instead. 'Well, I was,' she admitted. 'But I did stop myself, realising how foolish it would sound. And if you would like to change the subject, sir, so should I! I have been asked to spend an evening at Vauxhall with my cousins. My Aunt Caroline will chaperon us; will it be in order for me to accept?'

'Yes, that will be in order,' he said gravely. 'Provided your cousins don't choose an evening when you have some previous engagement, or when my mamma or myself are unable to accompany you.'

She shot him a horrified look. 'Accompany me! But, sir, if my Aunt Caroline . . .'

He laughed, turning his face to look down at her, his expression softening with amusement into something very likeable. 'Don't worry, Miss Winyard, I was only quizzing you! I am not such an ogre, you know! Any suggestions I have made are with your eventual comfort in mind, I assure you. I am sure you will be quite safe at Vauxhall, with your aunt and cousins.'

The rest of the drive home was occupied by his telling her something of the delights of Vauxhall, promising her a trip to the theatre and another to the opera, and reminding her that, when the season was over and the summer truly upon them, they would go down to Brighton for several weeks, for Lady McNaughton always hired lodgings there.

'And you may marvel over the Regent's summer palace, stroll along the beach, and even indulge in sea-bathing, if the fancy takes you,' he told her.

Back at Albemarle Street, Sherida found Lady McNaughton surveying with pride a number of calling-cards and an even larger number of invitations.

'I *said* you had made a hit, dearest child,' she declared, beaming at her protégée. '*Everyone* has thought of you! I declare, you will be so busy dancing and being entertained that we shall be hard put to it to fit half these invitations in!'

'I shall have to have another evening dress — two!' Sherida declared, leafing through the pile of invitations.

'You will indeed, as well as other things. And this afternoon, poppet, we shall go visiting, no matter how reluctant I am to waste time in . . . But I musn't be rude! I know I said we must visit the de Bourgs and the Frazers, but we shall have to go to Grosvenor Place, and visit your aunt Bertha, too. She and her son called this morning, and left a card, and she has scribbled on the bottom of it that she will be at home this afternoon, and would be delighted to see us. And later I want to take you to see some of my old friends, the Jerseys. Lady Jersey has given you vouchers for Almack's, and it would be a nice gesture to thank her personally, I believe.'

'Well, we shan't stay long with Aunt Bertha, shall we?' Sherida said hopefully. 'She is very kind, of course, but rather dull.'

'No, dearest, we won't stay longer than we have to,' Lady McNaughton agreed. 'Your aunt is probably rather put out that you are staying with me rather than with her, but your mamma was my dear friend, and her wishes are *sacrosant*.' She gazed solemnly at Sherida, then added, 'If that's the right word, dearest?'

57

'I think it is,' Sherida said. 'I know what you mean, anyway, and what a blessing for me, Aunt Fanny, that Mamma and yourself were friends! For otherwise, you know, nothing would have persuaded Aunt Bertha to come to London. She hates spending money on frivolity, and would certainly not have encouraged either Bertram or me to spend the season here. It must have gone sadly against the grain for her to have hired a house — or rather, to have persuaded Uncle Frederick to do so.'

'I have heard that Bertha was a dull creature,' Lady McNaughton said cheerfully. 'And I suppose she has brought her son to London so that he may compete for your attention, dearest! How lovely it is to be so sought-after!'

'Poor Bertram is only interested in Knighton Manor,' Sherida admitted ruefully. 'Or at least, Aunt Bertha is, which is the same thing. Whatever my mamma's faults may have been, selling land was not one of them. With each husband, she spent a deal of money on enlarging our estate, and I believe she actually bought land from Uncle Frederick, which was adding insult to injury! And now the poor woman is going to push Bertram into wooing me!'

'I've changed my mind, I'm quite looking forward to meeting this suitor,' declared Lady McNaughton. 'Is he handsome, as your cousin Roland is? Or merely masterful, like Greville?'

Sherida felt her cheeks go hot as she recalled how very masterful Greville had been the previous evening. 'Neither,' she said, however, striving for an airy tone. 'Bertram is only twenty-two and has little interest in anything but sport, so far as I can ascertain. When his father dies, he'll be a sporting squire.'

'Or when he marries someone with lands of her own,' Lady McNaughton murmured, twinkling wickedly at her ward. 'Come into the morning room, dearest, and have some luncheon. And then, when we've had a little rest, and changed into something different, we will go and visit your aunt and your cousin Bertram!'

CHAPTER FOUR

The visit to Aunt Bertha went off better than Sherida had anticipated. Her aunt was polite to Lady McNaughton, and though she sighed several times, and said it saddened her to see her favourite niece beneath any roof other than her own, she was more reconciled to her lot when Lady McNaughton told her that her sister-in-law, Lady Caroline Tilney, had expressed similar sentiments.

'Caroline! We've not met for years, but how could *she* think of entertaining my niece? I am sure she and Sherida have never met!'

'We hadn't,' Sherida admitted readily, 'but we have now! Aunt Caroline has two children, Roland, who must be in his thirties, and Diane, who is just a year older than myself.'

'I know about her children, of course,' Bertha said reproachfully. 'It is just that, of late years . . . But is Roland not yet married? I wonder why not? I must ask Caroline why not when we meet at Almack's.'

'Are you going to Almack's this evening?' Sherida asked, trying to hide her disappointment. She had no desire to be forced to talk to Aunt Bertha and dance with Bertram all evening, particularly as she knew her cousin despised dancing and would therefore certainly trample on her new satin slippers!

'Yes, naturally. Lady Jersey and I knew each other well, years ago,' Aunt Bertha said smugly. 'You and Bertram must give each other moral support, otherwise you'll feel very out of things, I daresay.'

Sherida hesitated, reluctant to make her aunt look foolish, but Lady McNaughton had no such scruples.

'Out of things? My dear Lady Winyard, you cannot be serious! The door-knocker has never been still since Sherida's coming-out ball! I wish you and your son could have been there! Such a success Sherida had! But there, you will see for yourself tonight that she won't lack partners.'

Afterwards, on their way home in the carriage, Sherida said curiously to Lady McNaughton, 'Aunt Fanny, I've never thought about it until now, but why don't Aunt Bertha and Aunt Caroline know one another well? After all, they are sisters-in-law!'

'Oh, that's an old story, dear. Your Uncle Frederick, who married Bertha, was a younger son, and so came into the manor on which they now live when your grandpapa died, your own father inheriting Knighton, as was right and proper for the heir. Now your Aunt Caroline was the eldest child, but by no means her father's favourite. She eloped with Roderick Tilney, you see. He was a charming fellow from a good family and he'd a decent enough inheritance, so it wasn't bad blood or impecuniousness which set your grandpapa against him. No, it was his

behaviour! He was a rake, but that could be for-
given; your grandpapa was a rake himself, from
what I've heard.

'Young Tilney was a gamester. He gamed
away a huge fortune and married Caroline when
his situation was desperate. He took her down to
his country property and got her with child, and
then began selling land. He would have squan-
dered her money in the same way, except that he
was killed, in a hunting accident, I believe. Or
was it a shooting accident?'

'When Roland was only a baby? Oh, poor
Aunt Caroline, how sad!'

'No, Sherida dear, of course not! Roland was
thirteen when his father died. It was Diane who
was the baby. And frankly, I think Caroline was
better off for her husband's death. She let her
estate four or five years ago, and is doing well out
of it. Then she came to London and opened up
the London house which her husband hadn't
managed to lose or sell, and moved in there. So
you see, my dear, it is important that Roland
Tilney marries well, for his inheritance was
wasted before he was out of short coats!'

Lady McNaughton's voice was artless, but
Sherida said frankly, 'Yes, I know. And I'm an
heiress! But surely Roland could find himself
someone richer than I?'

'As to that, I couldn't say,' Lady McNaughton
said evasively. 'But Knighton used to mean a lot
to Caroline. She was a girl of *strong passions,* your
mamma once told me, and despite knowing full

well she could not inherit Knighton, she always felt she should have done! She was a deal older than your papa or Frederick, you see, quite ten or twelve years. And for all her early youth she had been petted and spoilt by your grandpapa and told that she would be his successor. And then when she was in need, neither Richard nor Frederick would agree to sell land to give the money to her husband. She never forgave them. But time has passed, and now perhaps they'll forget their differences, and become friends.'

'Perhaps,' Sherida said without much conviction. 'But they're quite different, aren't they? Aunt Caroline manages everything for herself, and is very determined, and Aunt Bertha lets Uncle Frederick dictate to her, and scarcely even *thinks* for herself.'

'And yet Aunt Bertha has persuaded your uncle to hire a house in London for the Season, persuaded poor Bertram to give up the joys of . . . well, of whatever sporting activities he would be undertaking at home at this time of year, and move to London. It seems to me that both women get their own way in the end, though they have different means of getting it!'

'That's true,' Sherida said, regarding Lady McNaughton with a fascinated eye. 'And I am sure you usually get your own way too, don't you, Aunt Fanny?'

Lady McNaughton gave a delightful gurgle of laughter. 'True, my dear one, I usually do. In fact, most women get their own way in the long

63

run, as I am sure you will.'

The carriage halted and the coachman pulled open the door and held out his arm to help Lady McNaughton to alight. Sherida, following her out of the carriage, wondered what her guardian had meant by that remark. Did her hostess believe that she, Sherida, would end up marrying Roland, despite everyone's warnings? Or that she was attracted to someone else, and would bring the unknown round to her way of thinking? But Lady McNaughton was climbing the steps to the front door, her talk now of an early dinner that night, to allow them more time to dress for Almack's.

'A *most* important event in your first Season,' she was saying anxiously, as they entered the hall. 'I think, dearest, that you should wear the cream voile; it is a most becoming dress, and the amber slip gives it that touch of elegance which you young things don't *need*, but of which you think so highly!'

Despite Bertram's presence, the evening at Almack's turned out to be as memorable as anything Sherida could have imagined. The place itself could not but disappoint; the ballroom was decorated with large mirrors and beautiful chandeliers, but it did not have the fairylike beauty which Sherida had somehow expected, and the chairs, though numerous enough, were hard and uncomfortable.

Not that she sat down for long! Lord McNaughton solicited her hand for the first dance, and then Bertram, looking stiff and formal in the knee breeches, dark coat and white cravat which was the correct — indeed, the only — dress in which gentlemen might appear at Almack's, stood up with her for a country dance and performed his part quite creditably.

When she told him so, he said morosely, 'Aye. and so I should, for Mamma had me practising for days before we left Norfolk. And she was adamant that no gentleman could appear at Almack's in pantaloons. She said the Duke of Wellington once did so and was turned back by Willis, who said, "My Lord, you may not come in here in trousers." All I can wonder at is that the Duke did not simply remove them, and walk on up the stairs without! I am sure I would have!'

Sherida gave a crow of amusement, and a smile dawned on Bertram's countenance, too. 'Yes, Sher, but isn't it *dull?*' he said, sitting carefully down on a spindly chair at her side. 'I can't wait to get back home, which we could do in a trice if only you would . . .'

'If only I would what?' Sherida demanded, her eyes sparkling. 'Bertram, you aren't going to propose marriage the first time you meet me in London, merely to get back to Norfolk the quicker, are you?'

'No, no, Sher,' protested Bertram, flushing up to the roots of his hair. 'Though of course, I've always thought . . . that is to say . . .'

Sherida rescued him from his flounderings. 'Don't go and say you always thought we should marry, because I am very certain no such thought ever entered your mind! This is my aunt's doing!'

'Well, I won't deny she's mentioned marriage,' Bertram admitted cautiously. 'And I must say, Sher, that you've improved no end — got a touch of Town-bronze, as they say! Mind, you always were a devilish pretty girl! The trouble is that I've known you for ever! I can remember you when you lost all your front teeth, and when you were thrown from your first pony. And then you can remember me when I lost a fight against Tom Ferkin, and had two black eyes and a swollen nose, to say nothing of a chipped tooth, which I've got to this day! We're more like brother and sister than cousins, if only Mamma would realise it!'

'I know just what you mean,' Sherida said, patting her cousin's hand. '*And* I remember the fuss when you were sent down from Oxford before the end of term because of . . . a *light-skirt*, I think Aunt Bertha called her! And I knew all about Polly Middleton, though you never said a word to me!'

'Well. don't you say a word to my mother then,' Bertram said, looking harassed. 'Otherwise I will make a push to marry you, and you'd hate that, wouldn't you?' He grinned down at her. 'I say, Sher, do you know that little yellow-headed creature over there, in the pink dress?'

'That's Melissa Jennings,' Sherida told him obligingly. 'Shall I introduce you? And her dress is peach, not pink, you foolish creature!'

She led her cousin over to the little blonde and left him chatting affably, thinking gleefully that between them, she and Bertram would be more than a match for Aunt Bertha!

She had almost forgotten her Tilney cousins in the pleasure of being a popular partner, when she saw Roland's dark head above the crowd with Diane close to him, and Aunt Caroline bringing up the rear. She smiled at him, but at that moment the band struck up a waltz, and before Roland could do more than smile back, Lord McNaughton was standing before her, with Lady Sefton by his side.

'I have Lady Sefton's permission to solicit your hand for the waltz,' his Lordship said, bowing, and Sherida jumped up quickly with an exclamation of pleasure. This meant, she understood, that she had been accepted. Now she would be able to dance anything at Almack's without fearing censure.

She had been well taught, for whatever Lady Letty's faults may have been, ignoring her daughter's education was not one of them, and every young woman must be able to dance gracefully. But when Lord McNaughton's arm encircled her waist, and he drew her close to him, she found her breathing begin to quicken, and felt a blush steal over her face.

She did not attempt to speak, and was further embarrassed when he said mockingly, 'Relax, Miss Winyard! I have not the smallest intention of eating you alive, and seduction at Almack's is not considered to be at all the thing, I assure you.'

Heartened by the teasing note in his voice she raised her eyes to his face, saying innocently, 'Oh, I'm glad you've explained! You don't intend to eat me alive; but seduction, at some rendezvous other than Almack's of course, is a different matter!'

He laughed and so did she, twinkling up at him so that he said suddenly, his voice deepening, 'When you look at me like that, I have to remember I'm your host!'

'Why?' she enquired interest quickening her tone. 'Is it not permitted to seduce one's guests?'

'Miss Winyard, you are incorrigible! I hope you don't converse thus with all your dancing partners!'

'Certainly not!' Sherida looked shocked. 'Only with those gentlemen who promise not to eat me alive — *or* seduce me within these sacred portals!

For a moment his hold tightened on her as they whirled in a turn, and then he said in quite a different tone of voice, 'I see Roland is here, with his mamma and Miss Tilney.'

'Yes, but they've only just arrived. I've not danced with my cousin yet.'

'Well, when you do, just remember that nice young ladies don't mention seduction at *all*, especially to an experienced man.'

'And you remember that it was an experienced

man who mentioned seduction to me, in the first place,' Sherida returned promptly. She heard him laugh softly and she looked up at him, a challenge in her eyes. 'Well, sir? Would you deny that you began this most improper conversation?'

He shook his head, smiling down at her. 'No, I cannot deny it. There is no doubt, Miss Winyard, that you bring out the worst in me!'

The music stopped, and Lord McNaughton led Sherida over to where Lady McNaughton, sitting beside a fat, middle-aged gentleman, welcomed them with her sweetest smile.

'Sherida, my dearest, come and meet one of my oldest friends, Sir George Warrender,' she exclaimed. 'Sir George knew your mamma well.'

The fat gentleman got creakingly to his feet and shook her hand, exclaiming, 'How do you do, my dear! I was sorry to hear of your mamma's death, but this is no place to speak of such things.'

'I should have thought it quite an apt place, considering how mamma loved Almack's, and dancing,' Sherida said, smiling at him. 'Unfortunately she kept her two worlds quite separate, and when she visited me in Norfolk, she scarcely mentioned London. I gather the reverse was the case, too, so that I know very few of my mother's friends.'

'That will soon be remedied with Lady McNaughton to take you about,' Sir George said approvingly. 'Now, m'dear, you run along with

Greville and enjoy yourself. I don't expect you to enjoy the refreshments, because it's a paltry display as usual, with only soft drinks and very few of them. But the young don't need strong drink to keep them happy, eh, milady?'

'He's a good fellow, Sir George,' Lord McNaughton remarked as they strolled towards the supper-room. 'Have you realised what distinguished company you're keeping tonight, Miss Winyard? See that dark, morbid-looking fellow, refusing lobster patties? That's George Byron, the poet. And the woman he's with is Sarah Cottar; got a nasty tongue with those she dislikes has Sarah, but she's unlikely to sharpen it on you. And the woman with the hour-glass figure is Princess Esterhazy.'

'Fancy actually seeing Lord Byron,' Sherida said, staring at the idol of half the women in London. 'He's very handsome in a rather cross way, isn't he?'

'Well, he has worries, I suppose,' Lord McNaughton commented. 'He hasn't been married very long — his wife doesn't seem to be here tonight, though. Ah, here comes cousin Roland, bearing down upon us. Shall I let him oust me?'

Her hand, resting lightly in the crook of his arm, tightened almost imperceptibly on his sleeve and for a moment she was tempted to say, 'No, stay with me!' But where was her pride? She had been warned that Lord McNaughton wanted her merely for her estate, if he wanted her at all, that was to say. And he had been rude to her over the unfortunate walk on the terrace. Remembering all this, therefore, she said in a teasing tone, 'Haven't you had enough of my company, sir? I'm sure you are longing to chat to your old friends, or to the blonde woman who paid you so much attention at my come-out!'

He looked down at her, his expression difficult to read, then said lightly, 'Blonde woman? Oh, you must mean Caroline Lamb. She's not here tonight, of course, since . . .' He glanced towards the buffet table, then went on, 'But you are right, of course, I must not neglect old friends for new. Roland!'

Roland, who had been hovering, obeyed the summons at once.

'Would you like to relieve me of my fair charge, and get her some supper?' Lord McNaughton said with the utmost amiability. 'I must have a word with George.'

He went off towards the group still hovering around one end of the supper-table, and Roland took her hand and placed it punctiliously upon his arm, saying, 'Well, and how are you enjoying your first glimpse of the sacred font of fashion? Almack's may be absurd, but you have to be of a certain standing to appear here at all, you know.'

'Oh, yes. But apparently, it is the Patronesses who decide who is eligible and who is not, and they are by no means infallible.'

She was looking, as she spoke, at a tall, thin man with thinning hair and a prominent nose. But it was his costume which caught her eye, for in addition to the obligatory uniform of muslin neckcloth, dark coat and knee-breeches, he wore several embellishments in the form of jewellery, as well as a huge flower in his lapel.

Following her glance, Roland smiled indulgently. 'Oh, him! That is Lord Petersham, cousin. He is very rich and very eccentric, but of impeccable *ton*.'

She smiled back at him. 'Then no more need be said. Come cousin, let us have some supper!'

'If Lord Byron doesn't dance, Lord McNaughton, why does he come here?'

His lordship looked down at Sherida with an indulgent smile. 'Really, Miss Winyard, you know absolutely no gossip, do you? No crim. con. stories have ever titillated your innocent ear! Lord Byron used to come here to meet Lady Caroline Lamb, but now that he's married, he comes here to meet his friends, and very probably to be seen. Particularly by the young women, I suspect!'

'Oh!' Sherida said, taken aback. 'But Lady Caroline Lamb is *married,* and has been for years! And . . . and . . . *other* young women, you said?'

They were standing on the edge of the ball-room floor, but now Lord McNaughton drew her back from the set which was leaving the floor. 'Come and sit down, we can't talk here,' he commanded.

They settled themselves upon two of the hard

little chairs, and Lord McNaughton said, 'George's marriage is not a notorious success. And of course Caroline was married to William Lamb for some years before she made herself the talk of the town by flinging herself at Byron's head.'

How exciting it all sounds,' Sherida breathed. 'And is Lord Byron still madly in love with Caroline Lamb?'

Lord McNaughton grinned and patted her hand. 'No, little one, he is not! If you want to know what I think, I think George only loves George! And poor Caroline could not possibly love him after his harsh repudiation of her. But all that is past, and the stories which you may hear about George are largely cruel guesswork, so I should give them no credence, if I were you.'

'Stories? But what could be worse than Lord Byron making love to a lady who is *married?* And then coming here to meet other ladies yet again, after he is married himself!'

He looked at her gravely. 'Very little, you would think, but there are worse things hinted about George. And since he's a friend of mine . . . Come and dance, Miss Winyard. You've heard enough dreadful stories for one night.'

'No, I haven't,' Sherida objected, but she allowed him to lead her on to the floor to make up their set, which was just forming.

And when the evening was over, and they were driving through the dark streets in the carriage, with Lady McNaughton chattering gaily between them, Sherida reflected that she had never been more in charity with her host. How delightful he could be, when he chose! How much pleasanter her stay in his house became, when they were on good terms. She resolved, then and there, that however difficult he might be, it should be through no fault of hers that they quarrelled again.

For several days, this happy state of affairs continued. Sherida walked and drove in the park, attended the theatre with a party of friends, enjoyed several outings with Lady McNaughton and Diane, and was forced to buy a pair of silver sandals to go with a dream of an evening dress in white voile, embroidered with silver love-knots and with a short train of spider-gauze.

And then Roland suggested she might like to ride with him in the park, before breakfast one morning.

'Oh, there would be nothing I would like better,' Sherida sighed. 'But I've not brought a horse to London, and Lady McNaughton has not suggested that I use one of hers.'

'I daresay she has only her carriage horses,' Roland remarked. 'My own mother certainly does not ride in town and nor does Diane, unfortunately. She is not fond of the exercise. But horses can be hired, you know.'

'Yes, I suppose so,' Sherida said. 'Would I go to the stable myself and hire a mount, Cousin Roland, or should I ask Lord McNaughton to undertake the office for me?'

He said at once that he would hire a mount and meet her, early next morning, before the carriageway became crowded with vehicles and pedestrians.

That evening, at Almack's, Sherida confided her intentions to Bertram, who said wistfully that he only wished he might hire a horse too, and accompany them. 'But Mamma feels she is spending enough money, without adding the cost of a hired mount, I daresay,' he told his cousin. 'So there is nothing for it but to drive meekly around in the phaeton Father hired, and that is dull work, when you think of a gallop in the early morning sunshine, with the carriage-ways clear of fools!'

'You should apply to your Papa, perhaps,' Sherida suggested. 'He might have more sympathy with your desire to ride than your Mamma does.'

Back at the house that evening, she wondered whether she ought to take Lady McNaughton into her confidence, but it seemed unnecessary. She knew that there was nothing in the least reprehensible in riding with a young man in the park, provided she was not seen galloping *ventre à terre,* or committing any similar solecism, and she was determined to behave in an exemplary fashion. She knew that Lady McNaughton, though she had said very little, was not at all enamoured of her friendship with Roland; perhaps it would be better to say nothing, and enjoy the treat. And anyway, there was a strong chance that Bertram might arrive at the rendezvous as well, if he had managed to persuade his father to allow him to hire a riding-horse. Which would mean she was doubly respectable, with both cousins present.

Accordingly, she rose early and donning her new riding-habit, stole downstairs and out into the early morning freshness. The riding-habit was a daring affair in pale blue with black frogging *à la hussar*, worn with a tall hat, like an officer's shako. She thought she looked nice and as soon as Roland saw her, his admiring eyes told her she was not mistaken.

'Very dashing, Cousin,' he said. He was standing between two horses, and his groom was holding one of them. Now he indicated the smaller animal. 'Here is your mount, a quiet little mare, for you've not ridden in London before, and you will want to take it slowly, at first.'

Sherida did not wish to seem boastful, but she said hopefully, as they moved across the road towards the park, 'I do trust this mare is not a slug, Cousin Roland! I have been riding since I was five or six, you know, and as cousin Bertram could tell you, I'm a bruising rider to hounds, I am truly!'

Roland laughed indulgently, but soon realised that she was no novice, at any rate, for she held the mare in check easily whilst it was necessary to do so, and then, when they reached the first long, deserted avenue in the park, said briskly, 'Good! There is no one about to disapprove, so let us see whether my mare can go!'

The mare could go; she stretched herself into a canter, her stride gradually lengthening. 'I'll race you to the thicket ahead,' Sherida called, then bent over her horse's neck, seeming almost to wheedle more speed out of her.

Roland's mount, though a clear two hands taller than the mare, could not keep up, and he had the doubtful pleasure of seeing his cousin, clinging to her mare's neck like a limpet, draw level with the thicket a clear two lengths ahead of him.

Then disaster struck. They were slowing down in the almost tunnel-like quiet of the thicket, when a flutter of movement caught Roland's eye, but even as he turned his head to see what it was a small dog, appearing from nowhere it seemed, ran right under Sherida's mare. The animal gave a startled whinny, bucked, and then kicked out viciously, and the little dog sailed through the air, to land in an unmoving huddle on the grass verge, some six feet away.

Sherida, without a thought, scrambled out of the saddle, almost throwing the reins to Roland. 'Hold the mare while I see if the dog is killed,' she said. But the mare had been severely frightened, and she resisted Roland's attempts to bring her under control, bucking and rearing and squealing all the while, in a way which gave the lie to his earlier description of her.

The dog did not move as Sherida bent over it, but when she began to lift it, it curled its lip menacingly and uttered a little growl. She paid no heed to this, however, recognising it for what it was, the result of pain and fear more than a show of real affront. Settling it comfortably in the crook of her arm, she turned, to find Roland still having the greatest difficultly in subduing the mare. She walked towards them, but her mere approach, with the dog in her arms, made the mare show the whites of her eyes, and the lashing hooves warned her not to get too close.

'I think I'd better get this brute back to the stables,' Roland said breathlessly. 'My dear cousin, can you forgive me for deserting you so? I dare not let you try to remount.'

At that moment a voice behind Sherida said, 'Excuse me, ma'am, are you in some sort of trouble? May I assist you?'

Turning sharply, Sherida looked straight into the romantic countenance of Lord Byron.

'Oh, my lord, forgive me for not shaking hands,' she said, smiling up at him. 'But this little dog is hurt, and I must hold him gently.' She turned back to Roland. 'Off you go, Cousin,' she said encouragingly. 'I'll make my way back to Albemarle Street now, if Lord Byron will be good enough to escort me.'

Roland made off, still struggling to subdue the mare, and Sherida turned back to her companion, to find him eyeing her curiously. Suddenly, his brow cleared. 'Letty Craven's daughter! Am I right?'

Sherida laughed, nodding her agreement, then the smile died out of her eyes and she said anxiously, 'Do you know about dogs, sir? Is he much hurt, do you think?'

His lordship gently felt the dog's legs, shoulders and lean, shivering flanks. 'No bones broken, but he's bruised, and may have internal injuries. You can't carry him all the way back to . . . Albemarle Street, was it? You are my publisher's near neighbour. I'll summon a hackney — the road is not two minutes' walk from here, even for me.'

So with Lord Byron limping slowly beside her Sherida returned to the road, where his lordship hailed a passing hackney. He helped her inside, gave the jarvey on the box the office to take them to Albemarle Street, and after bidding him drive slowly because of the dog's possible injuries, climbed in and sat down beside Sherida.

'What caused your horse to shy, Miss . . . er . . .'

'Miss Sherida Winyard,' Sherida said demurely. 'It must have been the dog, I suppose.'

His lordship, who had turned so that he faced her, shook his head. 'I think not. I had the impression that your horse had turned its head before the dog suddenly appeared. In fact the dog almost catapulted into the roadway, or so it seemed to me.'

'I suppose he was chasing a bird, because I'm very sure he did not attack the horse's hooves, the way ill-bred animals sometimes do.' She patted the little dog's head.

'Perhaps everything just happened quickly,' he agreed. 'Now Miss Winyard, I've seen you somewhere before, I'm sure of it.' He appeared to ruminate, his dark eyes fixed broodingly on her face. 'I know! Driving with McNaughton in the park!'

'Yes. I'm staying with Lord McNaughton,' Sherida said.

'Indeed? And your mamma was Letty Craven! An adorable woman! I could write a poem to her eyebrows! In fact, I probably have.'

Two things occurred to Sherida at this point. The first was that Lord Byron's gaze was speculative in a way she did not quite like, the second that her mentor had told her that his lordship was a married man whose reputation did not bear close inspection. His next remark, indeed, confirmed her worst doubts. 'And I could write a poem to you, in that riding habit,' he said, his eyes raking her figure in a way which caused her to wriggle uncomfortably. 'Or out of it!'

'I don't think you should say things like that to me,' Sherida said, her face hot. 'Lord McNaughton wouldn't like it.'

This turned out to be an unfortunate remark. 'Oho, so that's the way the land lies!' He patted her knee and she tried to draw back, but she was wedged into a corner and the dog prevented her from moving far. 'I didn't know Greville had taken to robbing the nursery for his *chères amies*,

80

but since he has, I must discover for myself where your attraction lies.'

Before she could do more than utter an inarticulate protest, she found herself seized in his arms and ruthlessly kissed.

Sherida did not stop to consider why Lord McNaughton's kiss had stirred her so profoundly, nor why she found Lord Byron's embrace so distasteful. She used her free hand to slap his head resoundingly — she could scarcely slap his face, for it was pressed against her own — and then proceeded to kick him briskly in the shins. To add to his discomfiture the little dog, objecting to finding himself abruptly squeezed between his benefactress and her companion, bit him in the shoulder, and the jarvey suddenly shot back his little trap-door and shouted reassuringly down at them, 'almost there, sir and Miss!'

Lord Byron, doubly attacked, released her and Sherida jumped to her feet and stumbled down on to the flagway almost before the cab had drawn to a halt. She heard the jarvey shout but knew her tormentor would have to pay the man before he could follow her, so she was up the front doorsteps and hammering on the knocker before he could have climbed down, let alone fumbled for change in his purse.

The door opened so abruptly that she almost fell into the hall and Lord McNaughton, for it was he, had to step aside as she stumbled over the threshold and slammed the door shut behind her.

CHAPTER FIVE

'What on earth are you doing?' his lordship demanded crossly. 'I was in the breakfast parlour, quietly eating ham and eggs, when I heard a commotion outside. And then you emerge from a hackney, hatless and dishevelled, with a skinny cur under one arm. Really, Miss Winyard, you continually surprise me!'

'Oh! My hat!' Sherida exclaimed. Then, shrugging, 'I suppose Lord Byron will return it.'

Lord McNaughton had been striding back to his delayed breakfast, but at that remark he spun round, catching her by the shoulder.

'You've been in a hackney cab with Lord *Byron?* Are you mad, child, or just determined to ruin yourself? I told you the other night of his reputation . . .' He looked at her more closely. 'A riding habit?'

Sighing, she said wretchedly, 'Do look at the poor little dog first, sir, before you begin to lecture me. I think he may have internal injuries — Lord Byron said it was possible at all events — and he should be attended to at once.'

He took the dog from her arms, feeling the little creature's skinny body. 'I don't think anything is broken, and nor do I think he has internal injuries,' he said shortly. 'He can have my ham and eggs, for I've lost my appetite — that will do him more good than a medical inspection.'

He stood the dog down with surprising gentleness, and placed the plate under its nose. The dog, stunned by such good fortune, did nothing for a moment but contemplate the dish warily. Then, throwing caution to the winds, it fell on the food, swallowing in great gulps, cleaning the china with such energy that it seemed likely he might presently devour the plate as well as its contents.

'And now, have some coffee,' Sherida said, pouring hot milk and coffee into the finger bowl and placing that before the little animal. 'I think you were right, sir, he needed food more than surgery.'

'Quite. And now sit down, Miss Winyard, and explain yourself, if you please. I suggest you start right at the beginning, for I want a round tale, and no shilly-shallying.'

'Well, I went riding with my cousin Roland,' Sherida began in a placatory tone. 'He hired a horse for me, a gentle little mare.'

'And you were thrown?'

She followed his gaze. What with carrying the dust-covered dog, repulsing Lord Byron's energetic advances, and losing her hat, she could see how his misapprehension came about.

'No, I wasn't thrown. The little dog ran under the mare's hooves, and got kicked. I dismounted to see if it was badly hurt, and gave my horse's reins to Cousin Roland. But the mare seemed to go *mad*, Lord McNaughton!'

'I can sympathise with her,' he said blandly, 'for you have a similar effect upon me. Go on.'

'Oh, dear! Well, anyway, she wouldn't let me mount again, especially since I was carrying the dog. And then Lord Byron came up and said he would escort me home, but of course he could not walk all the way to Albemarle Street, could he, sir? So he hailed a hackney and put me into it. I did not realise at first that he intended to accompany me, and even if I had I should not have objected, for you said he was a friend of yours!'

'And so he is, but . . . However, I said a round tale, Miss Winyard. Carry on!'

'Well, then he said he had known and admired my mamma, and written verses to her eyebrows, or some such fustian. And then he made a very ungentlemanly remark.'

The silence from her interlocutor was marked. She added with reluctance, 'He said he would like to write verses to me too, in this riding habit — or out of it.'

Lord McNaughton passed a hand across his mouth, and for a moment she hesitated. Was he daring to laugh? But he said quite solemnly, 'Go on,' so she felt obliged to proceed.

'And I said he should not say such things to me, for Lord McNaughton would not like it.'

This time his groan, followed by a shout of laughter, was unmistakable. She stiffened, but he said, 'Don't poker up, little one! Can you not understand George's misapprehension? I suppose he thought — but there, he had no right to think any such thing of a young lady living under my mother's roof. And then what happened?'

'He grabbed hold of me and started to kiss me,' Sherida said crossly. 'And so I slapped him, and kicked him, and this dear little dog bit him, and when he let go of us, I got down and ran indoors —'

He turned from her to contemplate the table, and she saw his shoulders shake. In a small voice, which quivered despite herself, she said, 'It was very horrid for me, sir, and not at *all* a laughing matter.'

He turned to face her, his face grave once more. 'No, I quite see it must have been frightening for you. But have you learned your lesson *this* time, Miss Winyard? Did I not tell you that you must not find yourself alone with experienced men?'

'Did you not tell me that it was quite proper to drive with a man?'

He groaned. 'It *is* quite proper in an open carriage, you goose! But never, *never* travel in a closed carriage with a man. Dear God, a hackney, against which all little girls are warned as soon as their come-out approaches!'

'Well, no one said anything to me,' Sherida said obstinately. 'My mother never mentioned hackney coaches once!'

'No, because . . .'

'Because what?'

85

He walked back across the room to stand before her chair, an undecided expression on his face. 'Miss Winyard, when I first knew you were coming to stay in Albemarle Street, my mother and I talked about what you should know and what it was not necessary for you to know. We reached an agreement which I now believe was wrong. So I am going to take it upon myself to tell you something.'

She was gazing up at him with wide-eyed expectancy, but despite his declaration he seemed unwilling to continue.

'Tell me what, sir?' she asked, when the silence seemed to have lasted long enough. 'May I keep the little dog, do you suppose? He would be good company for Lady McNaughton and for me.'

'Of course you may.' He seemed to make up his mind. 'Miss Winyard! Your mamma was a very pretty and delightful woman, who married four times. And she was by no means averse to flirtations between marriages. In fact, Miss Winyard, it must be your first endeavour to make people realise that you are *not* another Letty Craven. Do I make myself clear?'

Sherida sat very still. It explained so many things. Lord McNaughton's attitude when first they'd met, Roland's taking her out on to the terrace, even Lord Byron's crude attempt at seduction in the hackney coach. And though she shrank from the thought, perhaps Lord McNaughton's kissing her on the terrace had been more in the nature of a test than a punishment. To see whether she would respond, throw herself at his head!

Well, thank goodness she had not done *that*. She pushed from her mind the sweetness of his embrace and tried to remember, instead, how she had resented it.

Her stillness seemed to worry Lord McNaughton, for he tilted her chin up so that he could look into her face. 'Never *mind*, little one! Very few of us have saints for parents, and you must have realised that my own mamma is far from perfect! But have I made you see, do you now understand, why you must behave with discretion?'

She met his eyes steadily, though her own were huge with unshed tears.

'I wish I'd known before,' she said quietly. 'You and your mamma have been so good. But I promise you . . .'

He took her hands and brought her to her feet. 'No! Promise nothing, and then you will disappoint no one. But bear it in mind, won't you? And now you'd best go to your room and change your habit, and I'll go in search of George and wrest your hat from his clutches, and take him to task for treating you like a *chère amie!*'

Sherida nodded, picked up the little dog and made for the door. But as she was crossing the hall she turned, and smiled resolutely at Lord McNaughton over the animal's silky head. 'We shall do very well, once we're both cleaned up,' she said. Then a real smile spread across her face. 'I must change my habits, as well as my habit. Good morning, sir!'

And she turned and swept up the stairs with a great deal of dignity for one so small, leaving him smiling ruefully after her.

For several days after her encounter with Lord Byron and the subsequent revelation of her mother's reputation, Sherida felt low and depressed, but such a state of affairs could not last, especially after Lady McNaughton had done her best to assure her protégée that Lady Letty had been, at worst, a trifle indiscreet, but by no means the abandoned flirt poor Sherida had begun to suspect.

'Letty and I were great friends as girls, though later, we moved in different circles,' she explained. 'I gather from Greville that he told you Letty was a flirt. Well, dear, I have to admit that she was, but then so was I! And perhaps because your mamma married four times, she was more at *ease* with gentlemen than most females. Gentlemen loved her gaiety and wit, but she never behaved in a way which should make you ashamed of her, I promise you.'

'Was she unfaithful to her husbands?' Sherida asked baldly.

Lady McNaughton winced, but answered frankly enough. 'No dear, never unfaithful. It was more *between* husbands, if you follow me. When she was *choosing*. And there was a period, between her second and third marriages, when she was what you might call *fancy-free* for two or three years. She was very gay then, and it made people think her somewhat light-minded. But you've no need to blush for her; it was just that when she was deciding which gentleman to choose for her *next* husband, she sometimes threw her cap over the windmill a little.'

Sherida could not help wondering how one could throw one's cap over the windmill 'a little', but after a good cry, she had sufficient common-sense to realise that whatever her mother's behaviour had been it could not have been really bad, or she herself would not have been welcomed to Almack's with open arms, nor found a great many very high-nosed ladies so eager to introduce her to their sons. In this she erred, but fortunately she did not realise that to a great many mammas, her fortune, her name, and her pretty looks were sufficient to offset any recollections of her mother's behaviour.

One other thing took her mind off the late Lady Letty; when Lord McNaughton came back from seeing Lord Byron, he brought not only her hat, but a disquieting story.

'George is in a great worry over your accident,' he told her. 'He says he got the impression that someone *propelled* the dog into your horse's path, in the hope, perhaps, of causing it to shy and throw you. Or it might have been meant for Roland's mount, of course. But if George is right, a dangerous trick was played upon you, which might easily have led to tragic consequences.'

'Oh, what rubbish! No one in their senses would do such a thing!' Sherida exclaimed, opening her eyes wide. 'Lord Byron is letting his imagination run away with him, and thinking himself to be living a romance, as well as writing them! You might tell him, by the by, that I intend to name the little dog for him. Beau Byron, I shall call him!'

'What, that mealy-mouthed cur?' Lord McNaughton exclaimed, temporarily distracted. 'I don't think I'll tell George any such thing.' And then, returning to the point, 'I must say I incline to your point of view, because it seems unlikely you've had time to arouse such enmity in anyone's breast here in London that they would try to harm you. But foolish tricks have been perpetrated by friends, eager to see one look amazed! I thought I'd better warn you.'

Sherida thanked him, albeit a trifle impatiently. It seemed absurd to think that anyone would play such a trick, and soon enough, the mounting excitement of constantly attending a variety of social events put the whole matter out of her mind.

The weather, which had been showery and cool for a week, suddenly seemed to blossom into glorious spring, and as the promised evening at Vauxhall Gardens drew near, she looked forward to it with unalloyed enjoyment. Roland had been attentive, but not embarrassingly so, and she found she could enjoy his company when the censorious eyes of Lord McNaughton were not upon her. Taking a leaf from Lady McNaughton's book, she treated Roland with an easy friendship, so that he found it difficult to place himself upon too romantic a footing with her without seeming foolish.

The evening of the visit saw the end of yet another fine, balmy day, and Sherida chose her attire with care. A sky-blue voile evening dress with a frosted crêpe scarf, a deep blue velvet evening cloak lined with lilac silk, and silver sandals, completed her toilet.

Roland called for her, and as he helped her into the carriage Diane, already seated leaned forward, eyeing her with interest. 'You look charming, but you've not brought a hat,' she pointed out. 'If it rains, your hair-style will be ruined.'

'My cloak has a hood,' Sherida said, settling herself on the seat beside her cousin. 'And my hair curls naturally, you know! Where is Aunt Caroline?'

'She's being conveyed to the gala in Lord Hammersley's beautiful new phaeton,' Roland told her, sitting down opposite the two girls. 'He's an old admirer of Mamma's, and was eager to make up the party! And besides, there would not have been room in this vehicle for six of us. We are to go next to Mount Street to pick up Mr Peter Unwin, who is to escort Diane.'

'You should have asked Bertram, and then it

would have been all family,' Sherida said, casting a mischievous glance at Diane. That young lady groaned.

'I know I said he bored me, with his perpetual talk of sport, but I would have you know, cousin, that the feeling is mutual — he doesn't admire me one bit! He said, in the course of dancing with me last evening, that he has always been overawed by *Junoesque females!* I ask you, what could be more insulting?'

Laughing in spite of herself, Sherida said, 'He's used to poor little dabs of females, you see, like me. But Diane, it's famous to be called Junoesque. I didn't know Bertram was conversant with such words! And *why* did he say it, anyway?'

'Oh, you know how *managing* my mamma is! She was talking to Bertram in quite a friendly way — though she and Aunt Bertha seem unable to bury the hatchet — and she turned and saw me and beckoned me over. And then before either of us had thought to invent a previous engagement, she told him to solicit my hand for the next waltz. "My daughter dances most gracefully," she said. I could have *died* of humiliation, Sherida, for Bertram looked *most* unwilling! Anyway, I said to him after we'd taken a turn around the floor that he had no need to blush for his dancing, for he was performing his part very creditably; and he said it was not that at *all*, it was because he'd always been . . .'

'Overawed by Junoesque females,' Sherida

92

finished for her, chuckling. 'Well, no need to take offence at that, Di! The first time Bertram danced with me at Almack's, he told me that far from regarding me with passion, all he could see when he looked at me was a muddy little girl on horseback, with all her front teeth missing. Or words to that effect!'

Roland, who had listened to these exchanges in silence, leaned forward, saying, 'I do have a certain sympathy with our cousin. You and he have been brought up almost like brother and sister, and it is difficult to change one's attitude from a mere brotherly affection to a loverlike ardour just because you are told to do so! If someone was to tell me Diane was not my sister, I shouldn't know how to behave towards her.'

'You might ask Lord Byron for advice,' suggested Diane, and in answer to Sherida's raised brows, 'Haven't you heard the latest crim. con. story from that source, cousin? Byron is said to be madly in love with his half-sister, Augusta!'

Roland, looking uncomfortable, said quickly, 'Diane, you shouldn't repeat such rumours to our cousin. Her guardian and Lord Byron are close friends. And besides, these malicious *on-dits* are not fit for her ears.'

The coach chose this moment to draw to a halt, and Roland got out, saying he would go and hurry Mr Unwin along. Sherida said cautiously to Diane, 'But surely, Di, Lord Byron could not be in . . . in *love* with his sister? He's married, and . . .'

'I shouldn't have repeated it,' Diane said. 'I forgot your guardian was friendly with his lordship. Please forget I ever mentioned it, because as Roland says, it is in all probability only cruel gossip.' She leaned forward, adding, with obvious relief, 'Here comes my brother with Mr Unwin. Not long now before we arrive at Vauxhall!'

Mr Unwin proved to be a thickset, fair-haired young man with a large Roman nose and a fund of amusing stories. But since he larded these anecdotes with cant expressions, Sherida was scarcely able to understand a word, and so sank into pleasurable anticipation in one corner of the coach. Soon enough, the coach drew to a halt and Roland helped her down, saying, 'Well, Cousin Sherida, there is Vauxhall, over the water, see the lights? Walk down here, and we will choose a boat to convey us across.'

'Oh, how charming, to go by boat,' Sherida exclaimed, and so it proved to be, for the sun had set behind the trees and dusk was falling, so that the deep blue of the sky, pricked with stars, was enhanced by the pale streaks of red and gold left by the dying sun, and the reflections in the water were truly glorious.

'There is Mamma — and Lord Hammersley! See, Sherida, standing by the entrance? Mamma is wearing plum-coloured satin.'

Diane's enthusiastic voice broke into the dream of colour and beauty which had taken Sherida's attention, and she waved to her aunt, who waved back, indicating the boat to her companion, a tall, middle-aged gentleman with distinguished silver hair.

Soon enough, the boat drew alongside the quay and they disembarked and when greetings and introductions had been exchanged, they set off, Roland having paid for their tickets of admission.

Without speaking, the six of them walked into the gardens, along paths lit by a thousand twinkling, many-coloured lanterns, past brilliantly lit booths and supper-boxes, under soaring arches and by slender, elegantly sculptured pillars, until they reached the principal grove, which housed the orchestra.

'Now, having looked about us, let us go to the Rotunda and listen to the music,' Lady Tilney said authoritatively. 'And then you four young ones may wander in the grounds until it is time for supper. Which box did you hire, Roland?'

They made their way into the pavilion and settled down in their seats, and while Roland impressed upon his mamma the number and location of their supper-box, Sherida glanced around her. What a mixed audience sat, listening to the music, but how colourful and happy everyone seemed to be! She was glad she had chosen one of her prettiest dresses, and had worn her new evening cloak and had not been provident and sensible, and worn something dull in case of rain.

When the concert ended, Lady Tilney swept

them out with her, and then she and her elderly admirer strolled towards the supper-boxes, while the four younger members of the party went on, to greet friends and to see for themselves the waterfalls, the lakes, the illuminated flowering shrubs, the statues and the temples.

Before they had passed the last of the supperboxes, however, Roland was hailed by a small group, already regaling themselves with plates of chicken cooked in a thick and savoury gravy, to judge from the delicious smell which wafted to their nostrils as they followed Roland over to the box.

'Well, if it isn't Tilney, by all that's wonderful,' drawled a fashionably-dressed young exquisite, eyeing the two girls with open curiosity. 'And Unwin, of course! Will you introduce us to your friends?'

'My sister, Jasper,' Roland said promptly, 'and my cousin, Miss Winyard.'

The young man bowed to them, murmuring, 'I'm covered with confusion! Harry, have you seen who's here?'

Somewhat to Sherida's surprise a dark young woman with a mass of curling brown hair and a magnificent figure, answered him. 'Yes indeed! You're quite a stranger these days, Roly!'

'I'm becoming serious, and doing as I ought,' Roland said repressively. 'Nice to have seen you. Your servant, Harriette.'

As they walked away from the booth, Diane whispered with a twinkle, 'That was Harriette

Wilson, Sherida, the famous courtesan! When Roland was wild and young, he used to mix with her set! But he's reformed now, of course.'

'I wish I knew people,' Sherida observed wistfully. 'But I don't, not yet!'

They were retracing their steps back to their own party when Sherida, glancing idly into a box full of pretty, extremely young girls, stiffened, and clutched Diane's arm. 'Just a moment, Di! I *do* see a friend. I simply must have a word with him. You go on with Roland and Mr Unwin.'

She went over to the box, and said urgently, 'Bertram!'

Her cousin, for it was he, turned round, his face slowly going scarlet. Getting up from his chair he came over to her, looking sulky. 'Sher, if you breathe a word about seeing me here tonight, I'll throttle you,' he said. 'I'm here by chance, for my friend Davies brought me.' He grinned conspiratorially. 'In fact, I believe my mamma thinks I'm dancing attendance on you!'

'Well, I shan't tell her,' Sherida assured him. Lowering her voice, she added, 'Who are all those young ladies?'

'Opera dancers,' Bertram said proudly, 'Pretty as pictures, aren't they, and full of fun and bounce!'

'Opera dancers! But does that mean . . . is it true . . .'

Bertram laughed, a trifle defiantly. 'Well, there can be little harm in it, Sher, for no one could keep an opera dancer on the monkey's allowance my father pays me, let alone four of 'em! It's only dashing blades like my cousin Roland, or Lord McNaughton, who can afford to keep little ladybirds like these! And in any event, I'm not keeping *my* eye open for a likely female, because . . .'

He was interrupted. 'Cousin Roland? I am with him tonight! Does *he* keep an opera dancer, Bertram? And Lord McNaughton too?'

Bertram shut his eyes and groaned. 'Hell and damnation! That's all it needs! I suppose Lady Tilney is here too, and her daughter?'

She nodded. 'Yes. But don't fear they'll tell tales to Aunt Bertha, because Roland and Diane never would, and Aunt Caroline is still in her own supper-box. And she isn't exactly on chatting terms with Aunt Bertha, is she?'

'No, not exactly,' Bertram admitted. 'There's no harm in my giving supper to these pretty little creatures, mind! It helps to take my mind off . . . well. Off other things!'

'Like me, I suppose,' Sherida responded, smiling ruefully at her cousin. 'Now you can answer my question. Does Cousin Roland keep an opera dancer? Or Lord McNaughton?'

'I doubt it,' he said, grinning down at her. 'What a one you are for taking a fellow literally, Sher! How on earth would *I* know what Tilney and McNaughton get up to, anyway? I'm not exactly in their set, am I? Now be off with you, or Roland will be over here, judging by the looks he keeps casting in this direction.'

So Sherida obediently rejoined her cousins, and presently they found themselves back by the box where Lady Tilney and Lord Hammersley awaited them.

'We've decided to remain here, and see the fireworks as they burst up in the sky,' Lady Tilney informed them. 'We're very comfortable, aren't we, Reginald, and we're sharing a bottle of port — most reprehensible, I daresay, but *so* delicious! You four young things run along, but try to remain near the edge of the crowd, so that you may rejoin us, if you please, just before the display ends. There is always a rush for the boats at the finish of the evening's entertainment, and I prefer to embark in a leisurely fashion, rather than be jostled down at the water's edge.'

The fireworks were to be let off at midnight, and already the watchers were gathering. Mindful of his mamma's wishes, however, Roland settled his small party a short way off from the crowd, on a slight rise where they would be able to see and enjoy the spectacle without getting hemmed in by other eager spectators.

And then, with a *whoosh*, the first rocket went hurtling towards the moon, and burst in a cloud of coloured stars. Sherida was enchanted. A set-piece was lit, and she oohed and aahed with the rest, her eyes growing rounder and rounder as wonder succeeded wonder. But then, for some reason, when the noise and brilliance was at its height, she had the oddest feeling, as though she were being watched. She glanced around her, but they were indeed on the very edge of the crowd, for behind them, only the pillars lining the wide walk and the bushes crowding close and hiding a tinkling stream could be seen.

She turned her eyes back to the firework display again, and then quickly, glanced over her shoulder. A tiny tell-tale flicker of movement behind a great, sweetly-scented bush caught her eye. Confused, she looked back towards the fireworks, in time to see a tremendous rocket rush skywards with a roar, echoed by a roar from the crowd.

As her eyes followed the flight of the rocket she moved to one side, the better to see it, and even as she did so she felt something bump against her arm, a slight smell of singed cloth assailed her nostrils, and simultaneously, a man on the edge of the crowd gave a hoarse, surprised shout, staggered, and fell to the ground. With all the noise going on, she would scarcely have noticed the man had not her senses been alerted by her own feeling of uneasiness. As it was, she tugged at Roland's coat, saying urgently, 'Cousin, that man is hurt! What has happened?'

She and Roland moved forward, to hear the man saying, 'My arm, oh God, my arm,' and then, in a stronger voice, 'I've been shot, by Jupiter!'

Roland and another bystander bent and helped the wounded man to his feet, and out of his coat. While Roland supported him, the other man rolled up the sleeve of the wounded man's shirt, to reveal a furrow of red, bleeding briskly, ploughed through the pale flesh of his upper arm.

'You have been shot, old Ned,' the bystander exclaimed. 'What the dooce is going on here?'

'You've been shot? Impossible, it must have been . . . oh, a firework or some such thing,' Roland declared. 'Who would want to fire a bullet into you, here?'

'Of course it was a bullet, I know a bullet wound when I see one, even though this is merely a graze,' the injured Ned said irritably. 'Good God, to have gone through the Peninsula War unscathed, and then to get one's congé, or very nearly, in Vauxhall Gardens!' His voice rose. 'Who the devil fired that shot? By God, my arm is sore!'

People were beginning to turn round and take notice, one telling another that someone had been struck by a firework, probably by a descending rocket stick, which, Sherida gathered, was by no means an unknown occurrence.

'Had we better go, and escort the young man to the boats?' Sherida said softly, to Roland. 'If the crowd panics, or even if we overstay here, we shall have a great deal of difficulty in finding a boat, from what your mamma said.'

The wounded man turned, and said thankfully, 'The young lady's got the right idea, Barny! I don't need help, ma'am, but I agree with you we're best out of it. Confound your infernal slowness, Barny, don't try to help me on with my coat for there's no bearing it, but go and search through those bushes and see who shot me!'

'They will have gone long since,' his friend said, but nevertheless took himself off, returning empty-handed at the end of two or three minutes. 'The bird has flown,' he said cheerfully. 'Now come along, old man, let's get you down to the river as soon as we can, so that I can attend to your arm.'

The two friends made off, having assured Roland and Sherida that they could manage perfectly well without any more help, and at that moment, Diane, who had been watching the fireworks and pretending not to notice that Mr Unwin had slipped his arm round her waist, joined them.

'Someone hurt by a falling stick?' she enquired, and Mr Unwin observed sagely, 'Bound to happen! Sticks got to fall somewhere, eh? Deuced odd if they stayed aloft, what?'

'That's right,' Roland muttered. 'Bring Diane along, Unwin, there's a good fellow. We'd best rejoin my mother and her escort before the crowd begins to disperse.'

Naturally enough, once they had gained their own carriage, Roland and Sherida regaled the rest of their party with the story of the shooting, and of how lucky they had been not to have been victims themselves.

'There are some young fools about,' Lord Hammersley said in his thin, precise voice. 'Young hotheads, who would be better off volunteering to rout Boney, instead of playing foolish tricks in public places. I suppose it was a firework, eh?'

'No, I think it really *was* a bullet,' Sherida said. 'It came close enough to me to graze my cloak, at all events.'

'Grazed your cloak? Oh, nonsense, child!' Aunt Caroline said briskly. 'Whoever heard such stuff? I thought you said the bullet came from behind you!'

'No, not directly behind us; it came rather from one side, where there were clumps of thick bushes. And I'm sure it wasn't a firework, or we should have heard the noise of it.'

Roland said quietly, 'I think there can be little doubt that it was a bullet. But surely it cannot have been so close to you as that, cousin! As I recall it . . .'

Diane then added her mite to the conversation, crying that since they had all stood in a tight little group until the man had fallen, surely it would have been impossible for her cousin to have been struck. A lively argument developed as to where the shot had been fired from, and Sherida agreed, for the sake of peace, that she was probably mistaken, and that imagination had been responsible for her thinking she had been bumped on the arm just prior to the man's falling to the ground.

But as soon as she got inside the house, and safely up into her own bedchamber, she took off her evening cloak and examined the part which had covered her left arm. Sure enough, the velvet was ploughed through by a burn mark about the width, and length, of her forefinger!

CHAPTER SIX

That night Sherida lay awake for some time, her mind in a whirl. *Could* she have been mistaken? Could the shot have been intended for the young man it had hit, or had it really been meant for herself? She could not help remembering, with a little shudder, that she had moved to one side simultaneously with the bullet grazing her cloak, in order to see the rocket better. It seemed too much of a coincidence that she should be both almost thrown from her horse and just missed by a bullet merely by chance.

And the shooting could scarcely be dismissed as a prank; whoever had fired that shot had meant business. She went coldly over the possibilities. The McNaughtons had known she was going to Vauxhall, so, obviously had the Tilneys, and Bertram, too, had known she was going, since he had told his mamma he would be dancing attendance upon her. But the McNaughtons had no possible reason to wish her dead, and nor had the Tilneys or the Winyards. Except that, unless she married Roland or Bertram, they would say goodbye to owning Knighton!

She was inclined to think that both attempts had been more in the nature of attempts to frighten her and send her running back home to Norfolk, rather than efforts to kill her. Why, after all, kill the goose who might lay the golden egg? But then commonsense reasserted itself. It would certainly do Roland no good if she returned to Norfolk. Was it Bertram, then, playing such dangerous tricks? She could not believe it, for he had the good sportsman's respect for fire-arms, and was much too aware of the dangers to go blasting off a gun in the middle of the pleasure gardens!

At last she fell asleep, to dream of being pursued by hidden enemies through Vauxhall, the sacred portals of Almack's, and at last, through her own estate at Knighton.

She was woken, late, by the maid Lady McNaughton had assigned to her, swishing back the curtains and letting in the sunshine of another lovely day.

'Good morning, Cora,' Sherida said drowsily. 'Is it *very* late? I'm afraid I wasn't in until nearly two o'clock.'

'No, and you never rung for me,' Cora said reproachfully, placing a tray on the bedside table. 'You should have done, Miss. I come up just after two I suppose it was, and you was curled up, sound asleep. You should have rung.'

'Oh, where's Nip?' Sherida said, disregarding the maid's reproof. 'I hope he isn't in the kitchens, worrying the staff for breakfast! And you've brought mine up to me Cora; what a treat!'

She uncovered a dish of lightly poached eggs, some buttered toast, and a pot of honey, and then poured herself chocolate from the little china jug.

Cora, laying out a green and white checked walking-dress, matching gloves and a green taffeta pelisse, muttered, 'Next thing I know, the mistress will be dismissing me for failing to put you properly to bed. As for that dog, Miss, I don't know what happened to him last night, I'm sure, unless Grieves, the footman, took him upstairs to his room. He's fond of dogs. Oh, Miss, look at the clothes, just lying on the floor! That pretty evening gown, crumpled all anyhow, and . . . what's this?'

She had been picking up the clothes which Sherida had thrown off with such abandon the previous evening. Now she held up the evening cloak accusingly.

'That? Oh, a . . . a firework caught it,' Sherida said with studied casualness. 'Can it be mended, do you think?'

Tutting, Cora examined the mark. 'I'll manage something, don't worry,' she said at last, folding the cloak over her arm. 'Fortunately it's near a seam, so I could either take in a bit, or try a neat little patch. Leave it to me, Miss.'

'I'm happy to do so, because I hate mending,' Sherida said. 'And Cora —'

'Yes, Miss?'

'I'm sorry I didn't ring for you. I realise it was selfish and thoughtless of me to allow you to stay miserably awake until all hours, suffering on the altar of duty.' She smiled bewitchingly, adding,

'No, but seriously, I *am* sorry. The truth is I was so tired I never even noticed Nip wasn't in his basket! It shan't occur again.'

Cora smiled back at her young mistress. 'Get along with you, Miss! Have you finished with that tray? Eh, dear, but you're a good eater, I'll say that for you! And now I'll take your cloak downstairs with me, and find young Nip and bring him to you.'

A quiet day followed, then Sherida accompanied Lady McNaughton to a card-party at the Lievens', and the following morning she met Lord McNaughton for the first time since before the visit to Vauxhall Gardens. After due consideration, she had decided not to say anything to her hostess, but she was not so sure that Lord McNaughton should be kept in the dark.

So when she entered the breakfast parlour the following day and saw Lord McNaughton eating a large breakfast, she was still undecided as to whether to confide in him or not. As it happened, he had his mouth full, and answered her cheerful greeting with a nod, so she felt bound to tease him by saying, 'I'm a little late this morning, Lord McNaughton, but so are you. I've not seen you since you spent the evening at Vauxhall, Miss Winyard. Did you enjoy yourself? Oh, yes, very much, Lord McNaughton! And what of today, Miss Winyard? Well, sir, I thought. . . .'

Lord McNaughton swallowed his mouthful

and said reprovingly, 'You are becoming a saucy young woman! But I wasn't going to ask you about Vauxhall, I was going to ask if you knew that the night you went there, Beau Byron had spent the night on my bed.'

'Beau Byron? On your *bed*?'

'In case you've forgotten, that is the name you said you intended giving to that repellent mongrel even now eyeing my breakfast plate greedily. He sat himself down on the landing after you'd gone a-pleasuring, and whined and scraped at my door until I was forced to let him in.'

Nip, sitting with his head intelligently cocked and his eyes lustrous with anticipation of pieces of ham fat, whined hopefully, making Sherida chuckle.

'Beau Byron, indeed! I must have been joking with you, sir! I call him Nip, as I'm sure you very well know!'

'Because he nipped Lord Byron, I presume? Well, having cleared that up, may I just remind you that you asked if *you* might keep the creature, you didn't ask if *I* would share my bed and board with him. So kindly keep it under control or it will have to sleep in the stables, where dogs belong.'

Nip shifted hopefully from foot to foot and whined again, then scraped a front paw against Lord McNaughton's boot in the hope of drawing attention to himself.

'Stop pestering, Nip,' Sherida commanded her pet, who took absolutely no notice. Lord

McNaughton absentmindedly cut another slice of ham and, equally casually, dropped it in front of Nip's nose. It never reached the ground; a snap, a gulp, and Nip's liquid eyes were fixed once more on his benefactor.

'I'm sorry, Lord McNaughton, but you shouldn't encourage him,' Sherida declared severely. 'Usually, if I am to be out late, I ask Cora to put him into his basket at about midnight. If I forget, I ring for her when I come in, and she brings him up from the kitchens. I suppose you were in before midnight?'

He nodded. Yes. I went to Watier's, but the friends I was engaged with arrived late and left early, so I did not stay either. And now you may tell me how you enjoyed yourself at Vauxhall!'

'Oh, we had a lovely evening, the fireworks were brilliant,' Sherida said enthusiastically. 'Supper, too, in those little booths! And everything so delicious!'

'And when you got home you were too exhausted to ring for your maid?'

'I *was* very tired, and . . .'

'Miss Winyard, let us not play games! My valet was asked to advise your maid on how best to patch, or remove, a powder-burn from your evening cloak. She told North that it was the work of a firework, but North doubted it very much. And then you tell me you returned from Vauxhall so tired you neither rang for your maid nor for your little dog. A tall order, Miss Winyard!'

All the laughter had fled from his face and his

eyes were too searching to be denied. She said briefly, 'While we watched the fireworks, a man was shot. The bullet, I believe, burned my cloak. The man wasn't much hurt, but he easily might have been.'

He stared at her gravely. 'And you were . . . ?'

'I was standing nearby, sir. Near enough to have been hit, I believe, had I not moved, the better to see a firework which was about to burst behind some trees.'

'Sit down, and tell me exactly what happened,' he said grimly. 'Exactly, mind, Miss Winyard.'

She considered for a moment, then went through the whole incident, not forgetting that it was at Lady Tilney's insistence that they had kept to the back of the crowd, nor that she had felt great unease just before the shot was fired and had, in fact, seen something move in the bushes behind and to the right of her.

When she finished speaking she looked into his eyes and for a moment, read murder there. Then the look changed to one of steady, ice-cold purpose.

'So. Someone knew you were going to Vauxhall, and took clever advantage of the crowds and the fireworks to try to shoot you. Is that what you think?'

'I don't *know!* I don't want to think it, Lord McNaughton! But it seems so strange — Lord Byron remarking that poor Nip seemed to have been catapulted under my mare's feet, and then this. And yet every particle of commonsense I possess tells me that such things only happen within the covers of the volumes of Mrs Radcliffe!'

'And you did not intend to tell me, Miss Winyard. May I ask why?'

'It seemed too absurd,' Sherida said lamely. "I think I *would* have told you, though, in the end.'

'I hope you would have done so. And I hope, in future, that you won't wait for me to find out that you're in trouble. Don't you trust me?'

His face was still serious, but she caught the ghost of a twinkle in his eye and was able to reply, 'Of course I do, sir! I trust you with my safety, but *not* with my pride or comfort! I had the horrid feeling that you might suggest I went home, or accepted no more invitations.'

'It might help in the short term, to send you back to Knighton,' he mused, adding, 'But on the whole I think it might be best if I let it be known in certain quarters that you have had two near-accidents, and that we are suspicious. That will probably be sufficient to frighten off your enemy, if enemy you have.'

'That is far better,' Sherida agreed approvingly. She drew a plate towards herself and began to hack inexpertly at the ham, so that his lordship, with a patient sigh, removed both joint and knife from her grasp, saying soothingly, 'The ham has done you no harm, Miss Winyard, so why mutilate it thus? Let me carve you a slice or two.'

'Or even three,' Sherida said, piling scrambled eggs on to her plate with a generous hand. 'Is there some coffee in that pot, or shall I ring for more?'

Lord McNaughton turned and tugged at the bellpull. 'One thing I will say for you, Miss Winyard; you have a beautiful appetite! I can't abide women who pick at their food.'

'No one has ever accused me of doing that,' Sherida agreed. 'I've been accused of being greedy, mind! When we were small and I visited Bertram's house for tea, he used to make audible comments upon the number of slices of cake I ate, and the bread and butter, too!'

'I can imagine,' he said dryly. 'And to return to our former subject of conversation, Miss Winyard, I think it more imperative than ever that I have prior knowledge of all your engagements. Do you agree?'

'Certainly. Lady McNaughton and I plan a shopping expedition to the Pantheon Bazaar this morning, for ribbons and other trimmings. And after luncheon we shall visit Hookham's library, to change our books. This evening we shall spend quietly at home, except that your mamma has bidden the Earnshaws to dine and then to play whist.'

'Innocent enough. And tomorrow?'

She wrinkled her brow in thought. 'Let me see, tomorrow. Oh yes, my aunt and cousin are taking Lady McNaughton and myself driving in Richmond Park. I've not been there before. And in the evening I believe we are to visit Almack's. Is that unexceptionable?'

He exclaimed impatiently. '*Which* cousin and aunt, Miss Winyard? Pray be more explicit. London seems full of your cousins and aunts!'

She laughed, but said, 'Why, Bertram and his mamma!'

He nodded. 'To Richmond Park, eh? And my mother accompanies you? If this weather holds you should have a pleasant afternoon.'

The weather continued calm and fine, and when Lady McNaughton and her charge climbed into the hired barouche with Lady Winyard and her son, all seemed set for an enjoyable outing.

'You are looking very charming, Aunt Bertha,' Sherida said as she settled herself beside her cousin. 'I don't believe I've ever seen you in a villager hat before. It becomes you.'

'And you look as pink and white as sugar icing, and just as sweet,' Lady Winyard said graciously. 'Now, Bertram, entertain your cousin whilst Lady McNaughton and I discuss the Cunningham's ball. Everyone will be there, and I am determined . . .'

The two ladies lapsed into enthusiastic descriptions of the gowns they would wear, the hairstyles they would prefer, and the jewels which best suited each material. Bertram, wearing an expression of long-suffering, turned to Sherida and asked her politely whether she had ever visited Richmond before.

'You know very well I have not, for I told you so when you asked me to drive there with you,' Sherida said reproachfully. 'Come, Bertram, you must do better than that!'

This made him laugh, and lightened the atmosphere a little, but there was no doubt about it, Bertram had not wished, for some reason, to accompany them to Richmond Park, and was, consequently, reluctant to exchange lighthearted chatter.

At last, under cover of the animated conversation from the elder ladies, he said in a low voice, 'Did you tell Mamma that I was at Vauxhall, but not in your company? If so, coz, you had better believe I'm annoyed with you! Such a storm in a teacup! Mamma ranting and raving and bidding Papa take stern action against me, and . . .'

'I most certainly did *not*,' Sherida protested indignantly. 'You may look elsewhere for your talebearer, cousin! Could it have been Aunt Caroline, or Roland or Diane? Or some other acquaintance? You were not exactly *invisible* in that box full of . . . of bits of muslin, you know!'

'Hush!' Bertram hissed, casting a horrified glance towards his mother. 'Do you want the whole of *London* to hear? I've been in trouble enough, I can tell you! And as for Aunt Caroline, it isn't she, for she and Mamma scarcely exchange two words when they meet. I made sure it was you!'

'Well, you were mistaken. Don't leap to conclusions in future,' Sherida said severely. 'Oh, is this the Park? How green and beautiful it seems after being away from the country for weeks and weeks.'

Presently, Aunt Bertha bade the driver stop and set them down, so that they might walk for a while. 'When we reach a comfortable bench, situated where it commands a good view, Lady McNaughton and I will rest in the shade for a little,' she said brightly. 'You young things must want to talk more privately, I'm sure. And you, Bertram, must make sure that your cousin stands up with you at the Cunninghams' ball!'

Bertram scowled and muttered something but Lady Winyard ignored him, talking animatedly to Lady McNaughton until at last a suitable bench was reached and the two ladies disposed themselves comfortably, waved the younger ones off, and proceeded to admire the view.

'Bertram, I know you don't want to marry me, but do you want to incur your mamma's anger when you need not?' Sherida asked presently, when the glade was out of sight. 'Why can we not *pretend* complaisance when you are with me? You could, in common courtesy, have taken my arm and smiled at me when we walked away from your mamma.'

Bertram looked a little conscious. 'Yes, but Sher, you know full well how I've always felt about you, and to be forever pretending don't suit me!'

'Don't you feel even the smallest *tendre* for

me?' Sherida asked mischievously. 'For shame, Bertram!'

'I told you the other night,' Bertram said, looking hunted. 'I'm fond of you, coz, but that's about the sum of it. And I can't change for the wishing!'

'I know, Bertram, I feel the same. But could we not go out riding and driving, once a week or so? And if you would stand up with me once or twice at Almack's . . .'

Bertram, looking supremely uncomfortable, said resolutely, 'Coz, I mean to tell you the truth! The fact is . . .'

He hesitated, obviously searching for words, glancing down at Sherida with an expression at once hopeful and guilty.

'Go on, Bertram, I shan't eat you!'

He took a deep breath. 'Well, the truth is, coz, that I *do* have a . . . a *tendre*. Do you remember Dolly Ainsworth?'

'Bertram! That girl who lives beyond high copse, with the carrotty hair and protruding teeth? There is quite a family of girls, isn't there?'

'Yes there is, you chucklehead,' Bertram said wrathfully. 'Sally has red hair, and Prudence is a meek little mouse, but Dolly is . . . oh, she's an angel, Sher! Golden hair, which curls so prettily across her forehead, and the bluest eyes! And she's well-dowered, Sher, and *her* father approves the match.'

'Have you told your mother?' Sherida asked. 'Surely, she will see that Miss Ainsworth is every bit as good a match as I! If I remember, she is the eldest girl, so very likely the estate will go to her, and in any event, if she is handsomely dowered . . .'

'I was all set to tell my parents when your mother died, and my mother promptly began to talk as though you and I were all but betrothed,' Bertram explained. 'I didn't know whether to tell her or remain mum, and hope she would go off the idea of you and I making a match of it. And then when she hired the London house, and began to talk of the Season, I did mention that there was someone . . . and she fairly rang a chime about my ears, I can tell you! Said I couldn't *jilt* you — such stuff, Sher, when you and I had never thought of marrying each other, let alone discussed it!'

'You'd much best pluck up your courage and tell her,' Sherida advised. 'She'll be pleased, Bertram, once she's got over the first surprise. After all, the Ainsworths have a very good estate, which runs with yours, and Dolly would be an ideal match. If she agrees, you must persuade her to take you straight home to Norfolk so that you may press your suit.'

Bertram stopped in his tracks, his eyes shining with excitement. 'By Jupiter, Sher, I believe you're right! Let us turn back, and I'll tell her as soon as we get home.' He bestowed a cousinly hug upon her. 'Good God, what a fool I've been!'

'So your cousin Bertram is going to return to

Norfolk to plight his troth with this young woman?'

Sherida looked up into Lord McNaughton's face as they twirled together in the waltz. 'Yes! And only think, sir, what a great fuss has been made about nothing, for it was just as I said. Once Lady Winyard and Uncle Frederick got over their surprise, they were delighted that it was Miss Ainsworth who had captured Bertram's affections. It seemed he paid a deal of attention a while back to a Miss Phoebe Sutter, one of the very beautiful and extremely ineligible daughters of a visiting curate. So you see, that's one worry off our minds — though they won't be absent from London long. Aunt Bertha intends to bring Miss Ainsworth back for the rest of the Season, to choose her brideclothes.'

His downward glance was enigmatic, but he said only, 'When do they leave?'

'In a few days. After the Cunninghams' ball, because Aunt Bertha had already accepted the invitation to attend that.'

'I see. And what of your other cousins? I don't see them here tonight.'

'No. They have gone to a masquerade given by some friends of Roland's.'

'You sound quite cheerful about it! I thought you enjoyed your cousins' company.'

'They're very pleasant. But *if* one of my relatives is taking pot-shots at me, I am anxious to find out which one. Now that Bertram is going to marry Miss Ainsworth, my only . . . suitor . . . is

Roland. While he feels himself high in my good graces, no member of the Tilney family is likely to put a period to my existence! But if he felt himself threatened, who knows? So to be honest, I find myself forced to be happy only when I am with strangers, and that will never do! Instead I am going to flirt with someone next time I am with the Tilneys, and see if another attempt is made upon my life.'

He shook her, gripping her hand so tightly that she gasped. 'You think Roland is trying to kill you, so you set yourself up for a target by deliberately killing his hopes? Why ask for trouble?'

'Something your Mamma said to me once made me suspicious. She said that Caroline was better off after her husband's death, and that he had died in a hunting accident, or a shooting accident, she could not recall which. So it is Aunt Caroline, I suspect, sir, and not poor Roland. Indeed, how could I think him guilty? He was standing by me when that shot was fired at Vauxhall. Bertram was with his . . . friends; Aunt Bertha I am perfectly sure would never dare to pick up a gun; yet Aunt Caroline, I remember my mamma telling me once, used to be a capital shot. She was an only child until she was twelve, you see, and her papa taught her to shoot and ride, as he would have taught a son. So I put two and two together, and . . .'

'And made five,' Lord McNaughton snapped, in a far from agreeable voice. 'But again, Miss Winyard, why *ask* for trouble?'

'What else am I to do?' she asked in a furious undertone, as the band brought the dance to a close and he led her off the floor. 'Am I to die an old maid just because I'm afraid of being killed if I choose the wrong man? Must I fear for my life every time I enjoy a dance with someone to whom I am not related?'

'You could try trusting me,' he said disagreeably. 'I'll take you down to supper now, and we'll discuss this further.'

But any hopes of a *tête à tête* were thwarted by Miss Eunice Huxtable, who pounced on them with a joyful cry. 'Oh, Miss Winyard, have you met Mr Elliston? He wanted an introduction to you earlier, but you were dancing. I believe you know Mr Elliston, Lord McNaughton — shall we go in to supper together?'

Mr Elliston, a tall, well-built young man with a cheerful, open countenance and a quiet sense of humour, proved to be an old friend of Lord McNaughton's, and they settled happily down at the supper table to talk over times past, and to entertain their fair partners. Sherida, eating and talking, nevertheless had time to assimilate the fact that Miss Huxtable's fine dark eyes were apt to fix themselves admiringly on his lordship's face, and found herself being even livelier as a result.

When they had eaten, Lord McNaughton asked Miss Huxtable to dance, and Sherida partnered Mr Elliston, who made her laugh by describing Lord McNaughton as he was when he had first met him. 'He was small, dark and evil,' he said with relish. 'A first-class sportsman and a keen cricketer, could swim like a fish and construe Latin like a . . . a Roman! But so conceited and self-assured there was no bearing it, for we were only eight! He'd been spoilt to death by his father and step-mother, of course, because of the accident. No one ever said "no" to him until he came to Harrow! And then it was too late — he simply *knew* he was right!'

'I can quite believe it,' Sherida said. 'But which accident?'

Mr Elliston looked a little self conscious. 'Perhaps I shouldn't have spoken of it, but all his contemporaries know the story. Have you never wondered how he got his scarred cheek? Poor Lady McNaughton was playing with him in the salon, swinging him round whilst he shrieked with excitement, I daresay. She was pregnant, expecting her first child. Apparently she fainted, and poor Greville fell against the hearth and split his face open. He was only about two, and the shock to them all must have been appalling, for Lady McNaughton miscarried of her baby within twenty-four hours.'

'What a dreadful thing,' Sherida said, much distressed. 'Is . . . is that why the McNaughtons never had any more children?'

'I believe so. Lady McNaughton never conceived again, at any event. But she adored Greville, perhaps the more so because she felt such guilt over his face. And in a way, they are on each other's conscience, for Greville once told me that his was the blame for her childlessness.'

'Do you think that's why Lord McNaughton hasn't married? Because he feels he could not leave his mamma?'

'Good God no, Miss Winyard! Nothing would give Lady McNaughton more pleasure than to have a daughter-in-law, and grandchildren! No, I think it is because Greville has been so very much courted, and sought after, that he has become over-critical, and suspects every female who smiles at him is his for the asking! And naturally, he knows his wealth makes him an excellent match.'

'His life is very comfortable,' Sherida said, nodding thoughtfully. 'He has his adoring mother to act as hostess for him and to run his house and see to his creature comforts, and his mistresses to . . .'

'Yes, quite,' interrupted Mr Elliston, with more haste than civility. 'I don't know if Greville discusses his mistresses with you, but you should certainly not do so with me!'

Sherida glanced up at him through her lashes, her mouth demure but her eyes dancing. 'No, he doesn't discuss his mistresses, and in point of fact I wasn't *sure* whether he kept any, but now I know, don't I?'

He frowned and laughed at the same time, then laughter overcame him and he led her off the floor and back to where Lady McNaughton sat with a group of friends. 'Greville said at supper that you were a handful, but he didn't warn me you were an impudent little gipsy, Miss Winyard! I'll return you to your guardian before you trick me into more indiscretions!'

CHAPTER SEVEN

'Aunt Bertha is back, with Bertram and his betrothed, Dolly Ainsworth. They're having a party for them, Aunt Fanny, and we are invited. See?'

Sherida held out her letter and Lady McNaughton, having pecked at a tiny portion of kedgeree and swallowed half a cup of coffee, pushed her chair back from the table and read the letter, nodding at the conclusion. 'Yes, I see. Well, we shall have to go, of course, but . . . oh, gracious!'

'What's the matter, Aunt Fanny?'

'The date! Let me make sure . . .' She reached into her reticule and withdrew a small engagement book. 'Yes! Dearest, I shan't be able to attend your aunt's party, I'm afraid. It is the same night as Lady Southgate's dress party for her daughter Elvira, who is to be married a week later, and I cannot fail her.'

'It doesn't matter, Aunt. I daresay Roland and Diane will be going, and will take me with them,' Sherida said comfortably. 'Any party given by Aunt Bertha is bound to be a cheese-paring affair, and one which I, for one, would not mind missing, but I can see that she would be mortally offended if I cried off, so I will go.'

'Of course, dear. And give my apologies, won't you?' Lady McNaughton said.

'I will. I'm meeting Roland and Diane later in

the park, and will ensure that they are going to the party, so that I am not without an escort. And then we may be comfortable.'

Though she did not say so to Lady McNaughton, Sherida thought to herself that this was one function which her aunt Caroline would not attend, and therefore, she herself might enjoy an evening free from worry. As it happened, it seemed that her surmise was correct. Diane assured her that she and Roland would not think of missing the party, and would certainly take her up in their carriage and deliver her home again at the close of the evening's entertainment. 'Unfortunately, Mamma will probably not come since she is promised to Lord Hammersley; they are going to the opera,' Diane concluded. 'So we'll enjoy a nice, silly evening, just the four of us, for Mr Paul Craythorn has been invited.'

'Another of Roland's friends?' Sherida asked, smiling at her cousin. 'How nice to have a brother who provides one with a variety of escorts!'

But despite the fact that everything had been quiet since the evening at Vauxhall, and she was beginning to believe that Lord McNaughton's words of warning had had the desired effect, she would have told him that she and Lady McNaughton would not be attending the Winyard's party together, had they not quarrelled sharply a couple of days before it.

Ever since acquiring her little dog, Sherida

had been in the habit of getting up early in the morning and taking him for a walk in the park or surrounding streets. He was a good creature, obedient to his name and eager to please, looking up at her with his bright eyes in his sharp little Cockney face, so that he reminded his mistress irresistibly of a gutter child, hopeful of pennies.

On this occasion they were walking along beside some small but respectable houses, close by the park, when out of them had run the prettiest child she had ever seen, hotly pursued by a man in his middle thirties, shouting wrathfully that she had best watch out or she'd feel his crop across her shoulders yet!

Sherida, seeing the child's pink and indignant face, stopped, uncertain whether or not to interfere. The roadway was deserted, however, and when the man caught the child and began to strike her across the arms and face, she felt she had no option but to intervene.

'Stop that at once!' she said in her most autocratic tone. 'Nip! See him off!'

Nip had never been bidden to 'see him off' before, but the struggle excited him, and he leapt up at the man, so obviously the aggressor, snapping and snarling in a bloodcurdling way, and then getting his teeth fixed in the tail of the man's coat, ripping it triumphantly half away.

'Hey! Let go, you brute! Call the creature off!' The man yelled, releasing his intended victim and trying to protect his coat from Nip's attack.

Sherida pulled at Nip's lead and he immediately backed away from the man, keeping up a low, rumbling growl the while.

'Leave that child alone, and Nip shan't touch you again,' Sherida promised. The man, muttering, moved away and when he was a few places off, turned and said defiantly, 'I'll be back, Lucy! You and Deb shall not treat me so! Have I not been good to her in the past? She was glad enough then, to . . .'

'Be off!' said the little girl, shrilly. 'You heard what the lady said! How *dare* you strike me, and chase me into the road! When Deb hears of it, she'll make you sorry!'

The small virago turned to Sherida, becoming a nice child once more. 'Pray come inside for a moment, ma'am! It was so good of you and your dog to rescue me! My sister will want to thank you when she gets up, for I must tell you she is still abed. And I must give the little dog some biscuits for being so clever as to tear Jack Farnham's horrible coat!'

Sherida followed her small hostess into the house from which she had lately emerged. They passed through a neat hall and into a reasonably spacious salon, with a thick, cream-coloured carpet on the floor, and ruby-red hangings and upholstery. It was a bright, cheerful room, made more so by a lavish display of silver and glass in a wide, bow-fronted cabinet, and by some pictures on the walls whose colours were so bright that Sherida quite blinked at them — but with admiration, for she thought them very pretty.

'Sit down, and I'll ring for Rosanna to bring up some tea, and a plate of scones, and then I'll tell you *all* about the despicable Mr Farnham,' the small girl said with relish. They settled themselves, and as soon as the maid, an elderly woman with a motherly face, had left them, the little girl broke a scone into pieces for Nip, and began her tale.

'Jack Farnham came here last night looking for my sister, but she was not able to see him, being already in bed. So what does he do but come in here and lay himself down on the couch, having decided to remain until morning, and to face Deb when she came downstairs! I discovered him scarcely half an hour ago, and told him to get up and begone. He blustered, and bragged, and then came at *me*, if you please! I tried to rap him over the head with the poker, but he wrested it from me before I'd had a chance to really crack him one, as I should have dearly liked to do. And then I had little choice but to run into the road, with him in pursuit, for I was sure he would half kill me after that!'

'You need a dog of your own,' Sherida said, regarding the child with a mixture of awe and amusement. 'Though you are very brave! I'm sure I should not have dared to hit a man over the head with a poker! And you are younger than I; a mere child, I should suppose.'

'I'm fourteen, and my name is Lucy Crane,' the girl said, suddenly remembering her manners. She held out her hand and grabbed Sherida's. 'How do you do! And who are you, pray?'

This made them both laugh, and Sherida said, still giggling, 'I am Sherida Winyard, and I am living just across the way, at Lord McNaughton's house, in Albemarle Street. I'm seventeen and am here for the Season.'

Lucy nodded her curly head. 'Yes, it is much the same with me. My sister Deborah sent for me in March, thinking me old enough to join her. I'm too young to become established on my own yet, of course.'

'Of course,' Sherida agreed. 'What about your mamma and papa? Do they live in the country?'

Lucy nodded. 'And now, tell me about your little dog! I would love one like him, to take for walks and teach tricks. Especially when Deb is out, and I am so bored!'

Nothing loth, Sherida embarked on the story of the finding of Nip, and before long, both girls were on such good terms that they felt they had been friends for years. Presently, their talk was interrupted by the entrance into the parlour of a tall, voluptuous beauty, with thickly curling brown hair, flashing brown eyes, and a carelessly draped negligée which left Sherida in little doubt of the excellence of her uncorseted shape.

She entered on a yawn, saying behind her hand as she did so, 'Good God, I never thought to be more bored by a man than by Ned, but he's gone at last, and . . .' She broke off, in some confusion. 'I beg pardon, Lucy, I didn't know you was entertaining a friend, or I wouldn't have burst in so!'

Lucy immediately broke into an explanation of how Sherida had rescued her from 'that wretched beast', with a detailed description of the gentleman's behaviour and manners.

The older sister curled her lip, saying disdainfully, 'That creature! There is nothing more disgusting, I feel, than a man who won't take no for an answer.' She turned to Sherida. 'Do you not agree? Miss . . . ?'

'I'm Sherida Winyard,' Sherida said with her friendliest smile, though she thought the older girl rather strange to enter a parlour so casually clad. 'And I do agree with you, I'm sure.'

'Yes, and she's living with Lord McNaughton, in Albemarle Street,' Lucy said, with a degree of awe and envy in her tone which Sherida was at a loss to understand. 'He was a friend of yours once, wasn't he, Deb? So generous, you said.' She turned to Sherida, her smile open and ingenuous. 'Is he generous to you, dear Miss Winyard?'

Sherida scarcely knew how to reply, for a most unwelcome suspicion had crossed her mind, though she could scarcely credit it. Could it be that this charming child thought she was living under Lord McNaughton's protection, as his mistress? But before she could speak, Deb cut in, looking very flustered.

'Miss Winyard, it has been a pleasure to meet

you, and I'm more grateful than I can say for your rescue of little Lucy here. But you must be off, indeed you must, before the flagway becomes crowded with folk doing their early shopping! Oh dear me, if Lord McNaughton ever gets wind of this there'll be trouble, I'm sure of it! What he'll say . . . but there, no need to get in a fret over what hasn't happened. Just you run off home, Miss Winyard, and not a word to anyone. Forget you ever came in this house, my dear, eh?'

'But . . . but . . .' Sherida stammered, feeling totally confused.

Lucy said vociferously, 'But we're *friends*, Deb, and I want Miss Winyard to stay! It's been famous talking to her about Nip, the little dog, and telling her about my own dear kitten, Fluff, and about the farm, and . . .'

'Lucy, believe me, but it won't *do*,' Deb said firmly. She had opened the front door and almost pushed Sherida out before Lucy had had time to protest once more, and Sherida found herself standing alone at the top of the three little steps, the door firmly shut and locked behind her.

The flagway was not crowded, indeed it was empty, save for a very elegant gentleman who was regarding her sudden appearance with a peculiarly saturnine smile, which spread as he fumbled for his glass, raised it to his eye, and gazed at her through it in a gloating and peculiar way.

Sherida gave him the most repellent look at

her command and proceeded to walk, with as much dignity as she could muster, up the flagway in the direction of Albemarle Street. She was sorely puzzled and unhappy over her sudden dismissal from the Crane household, but scarcely had time to ponder on it before a phaeton, drawn by two chestnuts whose appearance, had she glanced at them, could not have escaped her notice, drew up beside her, and a voice said, 'Get in!'

Glancing up, she saw Lord McNaughton glaring down at her, his face white with fury.

'I'm exercising Nip,' Sherida said defensively.

'He won't get much exercise in your carriage.'

He ground his teeth, she heard it distinctly. 'Miss Winyard, are you going to climb into this phaeton, or am I going to drag you in forcibly?'

'You can't very well do that since you've no groom with you, and if you let go the reins and climb down, your team will very likely canter off,' Sherida observed, but she climbed into the vehicle nevertheless, with Nip tucked under her arm. 'What *is* the matter, sir? You are white with rage!'

He allowed her to settle herself, and then clicked to his horses. 'I'll drive you round the park for a moment, Miss Winyard. This explanation may take some time. May I ask you what you were doing, coming out of the lodging of one of the most celebrated Cyprians in London?'

'C-c-cyprians?' Sherida stammered. 'How can that be? I h-helped a young girl, a *child*, no more, who was being beaten by a man, in the street! You m-must be mistaken, sir, for it was a most respectable household. Two sisters, Deborah and Lucy, and an elderly maidservant . . .'

He nodded. 'That's right, Deborah and Lucy Crane. Oh, Lucy may still be an honest maid, though I doubt it, for her sister has been speaking, I'm told, for months past, about bringing her youngest sister into the business. But Deborah, as I can personally vouch, my dear Miss Winyard, is an accomplished courtesan!'

For a moment, Sherida saw, through a red mist, a pleasant and satisfying picture of herself ripping every hair from the head of the sleepy, curvaceous Deb Crane. Shocked, she told herself hastily that it was moral indignation only, but she swung round and faced Lord McNaughton squarely, saying, 'She has been your mistress, I collect? Then why should it matter if I was seen leaving the house? I daresay you've been seen leaving there many a time!'

'Much though I hate to admit it, Miss Winyard, what is looked upon with mild approval in a man — I speak of a certain rakishness — is frowned upon utterly in a woman! If you were thought to be in the habit of . . . of hobnobbing with women of ill repute, your case would be quite lost. The *ton* would say you were no better than the Miss Cranes. Miss Winyard, are you laughing?'

'Oh, dear,' said Sherida, between giggles, 'and I thought Lucy had got hold of the wrong end of the stick about *me!* When she asked me where I lived, I said with Lord McNaughton, in Albemarle Street, and I think she may have taken it . . . that is, she must have taken it, that I was in her sister's trade!'

'I'm glad you find it amusing,' he said stiffly, his voice cold. 'I regret I can see nothing to laugh at in a young woman wilfully ruining herself in the eyes of society, just through a certain carelessness of behaviour.'

All desire to laugh abruptly left Sherida. 'What nonsense,' she answered coldly, eyeing him with dislike. 'How can I be ruined in anyone's eyes, when no one but yourself saw me?'

'None but myself and Lord Alvanley,' he said. 'I know of no one who will repeat the story with more relish of how he saw the little Winyard girl, who is supposed to be under Lady McNaughton's guardianship, coming out of the house of a *demimondaine,* before breakfast-time one morning.'

Sherida digested this for a moment, and then said defiantly, 'You mean out of the house of her guardian's mistress, don't you? Surely there is some saving grace in *that?* You could put it about that I was trying to convert the woman to moral rectitude!'

'Because I admitted to you that Deb Crane had been my mistress, that doesn't mean it is common knowledge amongst the *ton,*' he said repressively. 'I am going to drive you back to Albemarle Street now, Miss Winyard, and I must tell you flatly never to visit that house again unless you wish to find yourself packed off back to Knighton! And don't speak of this to anyone. The fewer people to know of this little adventure the better. When I leave you, I shall drive straight round to Alvanley's house, and failing that to Brook's, the Cocoa Tree, and White's, until I run his lordship to earth. And then I shall have to beg his silence! Good morning!'

It was because of the aura of disapproval which surrounded Lord McNaughton, Sherida told herself defiantly, that she had not told him about the party at the Winyards' London house. Although he had not been invited, she was sure that Aunt Bertha would have welcomed him in his mamma's stead, should he express a wish to accompany her. But at the moment, with the quarrel between them still an open wound, she had no desire for his company.

So she allowed him to suppose that she and Lady McNaughton were both attending the same party, and saw him off with relief when he left to see a pair of match bays which a friend of his was selling, out at Watford.

'Why have you and Greville fallen out?' Lady McNaughton enquired plaintively, after she had heard the cold exchange of farewells between them as her son left the house. 'I tried to ask him what was the matter, and got my nose snapped off for my pains! I've never *known* Greville so bad-tempered and difficult!'

'I got into a scrape, through no fault of my own, and he made me promise not to speak of it to anyone, but I don't mind disobeying him and telling you, Aunt Fanny, because I'm sure you are exempted from his ban.'

Lady McNaughton was amused and intrigued by the story, and told her charge not to worry, for since her son had been successful in running Lord Alvanley to earth, the story would not get around.

'The sisters would not give you away, I'm sure, for they're said to be kind-hearted creatures,' she said. 'There are five Crane sisters in London — six if you count your Lucy — and they are all said to be merry, kindly girls. Poor things, they live very much on the fringe of society, knowing all the men and none of the women.'

'Very enviable, I should think,' Sherida said.

'True, though it does not do to say so! And as for Greville, I daresay you've guessed that he is cross more because he feels guilty over his relationship with Deb Crane than through your unwitting error.'

'Guilty? No such thing! He positively *boasted* of the connection,' Sherida declared indignantly. 'And what business is it of mine anyway, Aunt Fanny?'

'Well, you did say that the elder Miss Crane mentioned he was a friend of hers, so sooner or later you would have guessed. I daresay I shouldn't say this, Sherida my love, but Greville is fond of you. He is probably longing to beg your pardon for being unkind to you, but he is so stiff-necked! So try to make it easy for him, dear!'

'I will,' Sherida said, her firm resolve to be horrid to his lordship until he humbly apologised for his curtness dissolving in the warmth of Lady McNaughton's smile. 'What time does he return from Watford? Shall I leave him a little note?'

'He may not return tonight. He and David Chillett are such old friends that he may decide to spend the night at Watford. But I think *I* will write him a little note, dear, asking him to call for you from your party, if he gets back before midnight. And then, in the carriage coming home perhaps, you may make up your difference.'

So Sherida set off for her party in a brighter mood than she had been in several days, nothing being more repugnant to her than a coldness between friends, even if Lord McNaughton, by and large, was quite the most bad-tempered, cold-hearted man she had ever met! Or so she told herself, climbing into Roland's carriage that evening, to be carried in state to the party!

'We're rather squeezed, but I daresay you won't mind that,' Lady Tilney's voice said, as Sherida settled down beside Diane. 'I hadn't intended to come, you know, but then I spoke to Hammersley, and he, dear good soul that he is, suggested that I join him in time for the last act of the opera, and supper at the Piazza; and then it will look better than merely making no *effort* to get to Bertha's little party.'

Sherida, who had jumped at Lady Tilney's assertive voice coming suddenly out of the dark interior of the coach, replied, 'I'm glad, Aunt Caroline. And is Diane to go on with you, to the opera?'

Aunt Caroline laughed indulgently. 'Dear me, no! A party of staid old people would not please Diane at all! But she will chaperon you, dear, when Roland takes you home, so all is settled.'

Sherida was a little discomposed to find her aunt a member of the party after all, but she speedily decided that there was little anyone could do to her in a house full of people, most of whom were known to her, and apart from determining not to wander away from her cousins, let her worries die as her anticipation of a pleasant evening increased.

For the party, which might so easily have been flat and dull, turned out happily due to a strange circumstance. The London house being a trifle cramped, but possessing some handsome windows leading out onto a terrace, the Winyards had been struck by the bright idea of throwing the windows open, ornamenting the garden and terrace with coloured lanterns, and inviting their guests to partake of an alfresco supper beneath the stars.

Miss Dolly Ainsworth, less mousy than Sherida remembered, proved to be a shy young woman with charming manners and excellent dress sense, so that many people, admiring her soft, golden-brown ringlets and white skin against the deep blue of her satin and gauze evening gown, thought her a very pretty girl indeed. Bertram was plainly deeply in love and very proud of his prospective bride, and hovered close to her, as though he feared to find her gone if he looked away for an instant.

Sherida found herself with Roland for most of the evening, which did not displease her. The longer evenings were upon them and the night-sky, which seemed a dark, velvety blue against the coloured lanterns, paled to a clear, singing green where the sun had just set, and Roland's romantic streak, which sometimes annoyed her, seemed more in keeping than usual.

A band was playing in the main room and several couples were dancing, and when a waltz struck up and Roland took her gently in his arms out on the terrace she felt perfectly in accord with him, the faint light from the lanterns, the scent of the flowers, and his quiet, almost pensive mood, all combining to make the moment magical. This sensation was heightened by the muted notes of music, coming to them dimmed and softened by the housewalls, so that the sound stole across the terrace like an echo from a worldlier place.

Looking up at the house as they decorously circled the paving, Sherida saw that there were balconies above them, where occasionally a servant or some other member of the household would appear, check that the lanterns were behaving themselves, and then retreat into the house once more. Huge earthenware and marble pots, planted with small lilac and laburnum bushes and other blossoming shrubs, lined the balconies and were spotlighted by strategically-placed lanterns, so that they enchanted the eye and gave up their sweet scents to further delight the dancers on the terrace below.

Supper had been eaten and people were beginning to drift away when Roland said he thought he ought to check that his mamma wanted to go to the opera. If so, he would hail a hackney for her and take her to her destination, returning for his cousin and sister as soon as might be.

'I'll stay here and enjoy the flowers and the dancing,' Sherida said peacefully. 'What a pleasant evening this has been, Roland, and how clever of Aunt Bertha to think of it!'

She was comfortably aware that she was pleasantly tired, and pleasantly full of supper, and that she had thoroughly enjoyed her evening, when she saw a familiar figure come through the long windows and stand still for a moment, dazzled by the house-lights and unable to see clearly in the comparative darkness on the terrace.

'Lord McNaughton!' Sherida called softly, and saw him turn towards her.

'Ah, Miss Winyard, I thought I'd come and see if you . . .'

He got no further. She saw a look of frozen horror on his face, then he leapt the intervening feet which separated them like a tiger. For one frightful moment she thought he had run mad and was attacking her. Then, he swept her violently to one side and even as he did so, she saw something large and heavy bounce, in horribly slow motion, off his shoulder, before descending in equally slow motion onto the paving, where it shattered into a thousand pieces.

She heard herself scream, faint and far off, and saw Lord McNaughton fall. His head was flung back, striking the paving with a sickening thud, and beneath it something dark was spreading across the stones.

The dancers had stopped and were moving towards them in the dimness, but Sherida had no thought for anyone but the man at her feet. She dropped to her knees, feeling frantically for a heartbeat, saying desperately, 'Someone, get a doctor!' and then, as she bent nearer him so that her curls fell across his brow, 'Greville, my dearest love! It should have been *me!* Oh, please God, let him be alive!'

Someone had the forethought to bring a lantern from its post in a tree, and shone it down on her. In its light she saw that the dark stain beneath his lordship's head was earth from the marble pot which had fallen from the balcony overhead, and now lay in fragments. Gently, she moved round so that Lord McNaughton's head rested on her lap. She stroked the hair back from his brow with trembling fingers, seeing the lids veiling his bright eyes, his mouth tightly shut, though his breathing was deep and laboured.

'What's the matter here? Someone said a doctor — Good lord, Sherida my dear, what's been happening?'

It was Sir Frederick, bending over them, his face pale and anxious.

'One of the marble pots from the balcony fell, and hit Lord McNaughton on the side of the head.' She paused, then said deliberately, 'It would have killed me had he not realised, and pushed me away. I was standing directly beneath.'

But his worried face showed only concern, and not a trace of guilt. 'My dear child, what a dreadful thing! Bertram has gone rushing off for a doctor and will be back soon, I feel sure. Shall we move the young man?'

Sherida crouched closer over his lordship's recumbent figure, as though shielding him with her body. 'No! I am very sure we should not move him in case of broken bones. Oh, Uncle, I believe he's coming round!'

So indeed, it proved. The head on her lap moved a tiny fraction, and Lord McNaughton groaned. Then a hand rose waveringly, and dropped again. 'Sherida. Run!' he said, on another groan. And then, 'My shoulder, oh, my shoulder!'

'Thank God, the pot cannot have hit his head, or he would surely have complained of that.' Sherida said. Then, as another figure bulked between her and the lantern, 'Who is that?'

'It's me, Roland. Do you want help to move

him into the house, cousin?'

She looked up at him, biting her lip in an agony of indecision. 'Oh, Roland, I don't *know!* I'm afraid of doing the wrong thing!'

Roland knelt beside her. He ran his hands lightly over Lord McNaughton's head, and said cheerfully, 'No, it didn't hit his head; not even a lump. But his shoulder is injured, probably quite badly.' He addressed their hidden audience, outside the circle of the lamplight. 'Here, bring a table, or something flat! We'll slide it under him without moving the shoulder, and get him into the house. Look lively!'

The silent ring of watchers melted away, to return presently with a trestle table. Roland had been examining Lord McNaughton's shoulder as well as he could, and now said, as he supervised the gentle and careful sliding of his lordship's still figure on to the table, 'I would say he's put his shoulder out of joint and broken the collar bone, probably quite badly. But he'll survive, Sherida, never fear.'

When the doctor arrived and began to examine Lord McNaughton, Sherida had leisure to appreciate how the accident had brought out the best in Roland, showing him to be both cool and resourceful; unlike Bertram, who had merely done as he was bidden, and then waited for further instructions.

Then the doctor said, 'Miss Winyard? Lord McNaughton is your guardian, I understand. Well, I am going to cut his coat and shirt off, to allow me to see this shoulder. There has been some bleeding, so the coat may stick a little, for though I did my best to get here quickly, there was obviously some delay between Lord McNaughton's being struck down and my arrival. Do you wish to remain and assist me? I am sure Sir Roland will not desert me, but I could do with two persons to help me.'

'Certainly I shall stay,' Sherida said firmly. She did not add that wild horses would not drag her away from the man who had saved her life at risk of his own, but perhaps her tone said it for her, for the doctor did not again suggest she leave.

'How did this happen?' The doctor said, as he cut away coat and shirt with neatness and despatch, and revealed a shoulder both torn and bloodied, the actual point of impact showing plainly with abrasions and bruising, the broken collar bone protruding through the skin at one point.

Sherida, steadily watching, murmured that a large marble jardinière, with a lilac tree growing in it, would seem to have fallen off the balcony, striking Lord McNaughton heavily upon the shoulder as it fell.

She saw Roland's eyes on her, worried, a question in their depths, but she said nothing further, and presently their attention was fully taken by the doctor's actions. When he put the shoulder back in its place, with Roland holding Lord McNaughton's inanimate form, and herself steadying them both, his lordship regained consciousness long enough to give a great shout of pain, but she could not help him even with a word of comfort, for he swooned again at once. She could only cry inside herself at his agony, which should have been hers.

Before Lord McNaughton could fully realise his plight, the doctor had administered a dose of laudanum, saying, 'Much the best thing that he remains unconscious while I set the bone and clean the wound. Then he will sleep naturally.'

Sherida watched as he set the broken bone, with a neatness which she regarded with approval, and dusted the cleaned wound with basilicum powder. When it had been bandaged, and Lord McNaughton had been tenderly inserted into one of Bertram's clean nightshirts, the doctor said, 'He'll do now! I wanted him on this table to set the bone, but now we'll use it to convey him to his room. Would you ask Lady Winyard where he is to stay, Miss Winyard?'

'Oh, he cannot stay here,' Sherida said at once. 'He must be brought home!'

'He cannot be moved, perhaps for several days,' the doctor said equally firmly. 'But I'm sure Lady Winyard will find a comfortable bed-chamber for him.'

Sherida looked at the doctor's sensible face, then at Lord McNaughton's countenance, drained of colour and, apparently, of life. 'I . . . yes, I understand. But I shall remain here with him until his mother gets here.' She turned to her cousin. 'Roland, could you get someone to send a message to Lady McNaughton, saying that her son has been injured, but that he will be safely cared for tonight? And would you ask her to send Cora here, so that we may look after Lord McNaughton together?'

'Certainly,' Roland assented, standing in the doorway ready to see the doctor away. 'Shall I ask Cora to pack you a bag, with your night-clothes and so on inside?'

'If you please. And a change of clothing too, for I can scarcely go home tomorrow morning in my evening gown! Oh, and Roland, a flask of lavender water, and my copy of *Evelina*, which is beside my bed. And you'd best tell her to bring Nip, too.'

'Your little dog? Whatever for?'

'Because he will fret if he's left alone all night, with neither Cora nor myself,' Sherida said. 'And Roland, tell Cora to hurry!'

He turned in the doorway, in the act of ushering the doctor into the hall. 'Don't worry, cousin, I shall bring her back to you myself. And now I must go and find Lady Winyard, and discuss with her where best Lord McNaughton should lie tonight.'

'But what about moving him?' Sherida asked. 'Can you wait until he has been moved, Roland, for I don't think Bertram and Uncle Frederick would be gentle enough.'

The doctor, who had stood patiently by while the discussion took place, now intervened.

'Young lady,' he said, looking intently at Sherida, 'you have been a great help, and very sensible; but you must allow me some discretion of my own! I shall *personally* supervise the moving of my patient, and shall see him comfortably settled before I leave this house. Does that satisfy you?'

'Oh, yes, completely,' Sherida said fervently. 'Please forgive me if I seem over-anxious, but . . . I don't know if you realise that Lord McNaughton saved *me* from almost certain death at his own expense? It was I who was standing directly in the path of the marble pot which fell from the balcony, and Lord McNaughton saw, and dived across to push me to safety.'

'No, I did not realise. Then I will allow you to indulge in a few nervous fears,' the doctor said, smiling comfortingly at her. 'What a dreadful experience for you, Miss Winyard! Would you like me to mix you something to calm your nerves?'

'No, thank you, for it would undoubtedly cause me to fall asleep, and I wish to remain awake,' Sherida said frankly. 'It is the least I can do.'

He did not demur, but nodded, obviously understanding her feelings. 'Very well. I shall visit our patient again in the morning. Should he wake and grow feverish, or be in much pain, I will leave you a draught for him.'

True to his promise, he saw Lord McNaughton safely bestowed in a large double bed in a pleasant bedchamber, with a fire burning on the hearth and his medicines standing conveniently near the bed, before leaving Sherida alone with her patient.

Bertram came up, hovering about the room, anxious to help, but was driven off by Sherida reminding him that his first duty must be to Miss Ainsworth, whose delicate sensibilities had been quite overset by the accident.

Lady Winyard popped her head round the door, to say in a subdued voice that she would bring a pan of milk up presently, for Sherida to warm if necessary. 'I wish I could help you, dear,' she said faintly, 'but I could not nurse him; when I think of the pain he must have suffered, I feel quite queasy! I'll bring the milk later.'

And with her departure, Sherida settled down to her vigil.

CHAPTER EIGHT

For the first twenty minutes, she was content merely to scrutinise Lord McNaughton's face. The lines of it, so austere now that the light of his eyes was hooded from her, yet so familiar, so dear to her! She followed the line of his thick brows, the slash of the scar, the curve of his lashes, lying motionless on his pale skin. His lips, in repose, showed humour in the short upper lip, and both generosity and sensuality in the full lower one.

How had she not realised that she loved him? she marvelled. She had thought him autocratic, selfish, aggressive. She thought so still, she realised, with a chuckle at herself, for a person's nature did not change in two minutes. But she had known, from the moment that she had seen him fall unconscious at her feet and had thought for one appalled moment that he was dead and lost to her forever, that she loved him. He had saved her life, and without him, her life would not be worth saving!

Presently, as though her eyes upon him were felt through the layers of unconsciousness, the fumes of laudanum, he moved a little, muttering something, and a lock of his thick hair fell across his forehead. Instinctively she reached out and smoothed it back, and as she did so, his eyes opened. Dark, pain-filled eyes, smoky with the drug and with no recognition in their depths, yet his glance sent a shaft of joy through her.

'Lord McNaughton, you must lie still, for your shoulder is broken,' she whispered. 'The doctor says you must sleep.'

His eyes dwelt on her face as though he strove to focus on her features, then he said in a slurred monotone, 'Run, run away! Don't stay here, it is falling!'

She knelt by the bed, her face only inches from his. 'We're both safe,' she said distinctly. 'It has fallen, and we are both alive! The danger has gone. Sleep now, Greville.'

She had used his name instinctively, straining after something which would bring him peace of mind, and it worked. He gave a long, satisfied sigh, and slowly the heavy lids drooped until the lashes lay once more on his cheeks, and he slept.

Sherida drew back from the bed a little. Cora would be here soon, and then she could help her to raise his lordship to swallow the doctor's draught, should he wake again. If not, he would do very well to sleep until morning.

A soft tap on the door brought her head round quickly. Could it be Cora already? But it was only Aunt Bertha, with a jug of milk, a small pan, and two cups of hot milk and some biscuits.

'I've brought you a drink of milk and some biscuits,' she whispered. 'I brought a second cup for Lord McNaughton, but I see he's sleeping still. Poor young man, what a terrible thing! And on such a happy occasion, too. I cannot but feel guilty, though I checked those pots most carefully myself, and would have sworn they were safe.'

Lady Winyard stood looking down at his lordship, awe and distress evident on her mousy little face. 'I dread facing Lady McNaughton,' she went on. 'She is so fond of her son, and must think me a careless creature.'

'Nonsense, Aunt,' Sherida said bracingly. 'Come and sit down and drink the second cup of milk whilst I drink mine! Now why should Lady McNaughton think you careless?'

'She should not! Indeed, your Aunt Caroline would confirm that I checked the pots myself not twenty minutes before the accident.'

'Aunt Caroline? How came she to be involved?'

'Not exactly involved, Sherida dear, but interested! She is going to give a masquerade for Diane, later in the season — though not too late, when all the world is at Brighton! She commented to me upon how cleverly the lamps had been arranged so that the blooms were thrown into prominence, and I took her upstairs so that she could see for herself how it was done.'

'Indeed?'

'Oh, yes, and she greatly admired the display. She said she might very well do something similar at her masquerade, for it would allow her to use her terrace, and thus double the number of guests. She thought a marquee, perhaps, put up in the garden in case of rain! But anyway, the pots were secure enough then. So I left Caroline there, and . . .'

'You left her?' Sherida said sharply. 'Upstairs, Aunt Bertha?'

'Yes. She had the headache, and wanted to freshen up and bathe her forehead with cologne. I believe she was going on somewhere else,' Lady Winyard said vaguely. 'I showed her into my bedchamber, and left her. I could not remain with her, of course, for I had a great many other guests to attend to!'

'Of course,' Sherida said automatically. 'You must not blame yourself anyway, Aunt Bertha. And now you'd best go off to bed, or you will be unable to wake up in the morning!'

'Very well, dear, if you are sure you'll be all right,' Aunt Bertha said. She got to her feet, kissed Sherida's cheek, hissed her goodnights in deference to Lord McNaughton's unstirring slumber, and tiptoed out of the room.

Cora's quiet arrival, with Nip on his leash, was the next thing to bring her out of her chair; she soothed Nip's exuberant greetings, told Cora to sit down in the comfortable wing-chair by the fire, and settled herself beside the bed once more.

And then, for some hours, she just watched over Lord McNaughton's slumber.

His first stirring and wakening came in the early hours. He was hot, restless, and in considerable pain. He was disinclined to take more laudanum, which he said was the main cause of his headache, and disinclined, also, to drink the paregoric draught the doctor had left.

'You should never have come to the party without my mother,' he said crossly, wincing as he turned his head to look at her. 'I found mamma's note and came to bring you home, so that Roland would not have to go out of his way, and . . .'

'I know it's all my fault,' Sherida confessed miserably. Despite her resolve to be firm with him, tears formed in her eyes and ran unchecked down her cheeks. 'It should have been *I* who had the broken shoulder, at the very least. But indeed, Lord McNaughton, you must take your medicine!'

He put out his good hand, and pulled her wrist so that she knelt again by the bed. 'Stop crying, you foolish child,' he said gruffly. 'It wasn't your fault, exactly! I daresay it would have happened just the same, had I *and* my mother been present. There! Is that not handsome of me?'

Sherida smiled through her tears. 'Very handsome; practically an apology, which I never thought to hear from *you*, sir!'

He smiled, but so wearily that her heart ached for him. 'Impudent, Miss Winyard! Oh, curse this shoulder!'

She glanced round at Cora, stirring in the wing-chair, then turned back to the bed. 'Lord McNaughton, I am going to help you up a little, and then you must swallow your medicine. Otherwise Cora and I shall have to tip it down your throat, and you won't like that one bit, for I am very unhandy and shall probably get it all over the bed as well.'

He said urgently, 'No, wait a minute! What of the accident? Quick, before your woman wakes. Tell me what happened.'

'I don't *know!* Aunt Bertha left Aunt Caroline upstairs, she says, and when she came down the pots were secure enough. But it could have been anyone, even Roland had left me, to find his mother and sister. And Bertram wasn't on the terrace either!'

'I see. Then you must continue to treat me with coldness, Miss Winyard.'

She said, with an iciness which had nothing to do with his command, 'And when have I treated you otherwise?'

'Greville, my dearest love, it should have been *me,*' he quoted, his glance slightly questioning, slightly mischievous.

Sherida, scarlet to the roots of her hair, said dampingly, 'That, sir, *must* be the wild ravings of your delirium! You cannot have seriously believed me to have said something so . . . so . . .'

He reached out his hand gropingly, and she allowed him to pat her arm, though her face was set and her eyes stormy. 'My dear . . . Miss Winyard, we must needs be at loggerheads until we have settled this business.'

She said through clenched teeth, 'That will suit me admirably, for a more detestable, conceited . . . And furthermore, sir, you *will* take your medicine!'

Without further ado she pushed another

pillow down behind him, and tipped a dose of medicine into a small glass. He said, 'If you would but support my head on your arm, I could take it more . . .' And then the words were lost in splutters as she tilted the dose ruthlessly down his throat.

That done, she removed the pillow, briskly settled him in the bed, tucked him in so firmly that he was moved to complain, and went and sat opposite Cora beside the fire, her breast still heaving with emotion.

Of all the hateful men she had ever met, she told herself as she saw him settle into slumber once more, Lord McNaughton, without any doubt whatsoever, took the palm! And as for loving him . . . !

'Fortunately, your lordship has an excellent constitution; in short, you're as strong as an ox,' the doctor observed severely after the invalid had been confined to his room for three days. 'Otherwise this accident might have had a very different ending! And you have had most careful and devoted nursing.' He smiled at Sherida and at Lady McNaughton, who had shared the burden of keeping his lordship abed for most of that time.

'Oh, *most* careful nursing,' Lord McNaughton said. 'Miss Winyard forces medicine down my throat with all the care and devotion of one stuffing a reluctant cushion! And my dearest mamma encourages her!'

'Merely carrying out my orders, my dear sir,' the doctor said jovially. 'And now I think you will be pleased to learn that you may go home. But you *must* go slowly at first, Lord McNaughton! Plenty of rest, gentle exercise, and good food and sleep; that's my prescription for the next few weeks. And then you'll find the bone has mended as good as new, and you will be able to ride and drive with impunity.'

'Very well,' Lord McNaughton growled ungraciously. 'Though what harm could be done by driving myself gently. . . .'

'If the bone parts, I'll not be answerable for the consequences,' the doctor told him severely. 'You could have restricted movement, or none at all, in that arm for the rest of your life. And pretty well constant pain, what is more. You don't want to become a cripple for want of a little patience, do you?'

'Of course he doesn't,' Lady McNaughton cut in, holding out her hand to the doctor. 'Good day to you, Dr Rayner, and thank you very much for bearing with my son! I trust you will call upon us in a day or so, to see how the shoulder goes on?'

'Of course I shall, your ladyship,' the doctor responded, much gratified. 'Good day to you, ma'am; Miss Winyard, your lordship.'

He bowed himself out and the two women looked at each other meaningfully behind Lord McNaughton's back, as he stood looking down into the square below. They had been obliged to

157

keep him in bed three days, and today was his first day on his feet; he had been a difficult patient, eager to be up, reluctant to take his medicine, suspicious that every hot drink might contain laudanum, of which he disapproved. But now, at last, he would be able to return home so that he might prowl the house, dictate letters in his study, call for his staff to do his bidding, instead of making his mother and ward the sole recipients of all his irritably pent-up energy.

'Well, Greville dear, do you think you should put on your coat and come downstairs, and thank Lady Winyard for her hospitality these past three days?' Lady McNaughton said at last, turning to her son. 'And then, since Cora has gone for the carriage, I think we might leave!'

Lord McNaughton turned at that, a grin spreading across his face. 'Poor mamma, have I been a great trial to you? I'm not a good invalid, am I? And Miss Winyard has had to bear a share of my crotchets too. I apologise to both of you, unreservedly! And one day, dear Mamma, I will explain more fully than I am able to now, just *why* I have been so difficult. But for the present, let us indeed go and bid Lady Winyard farewell, and get back to Albemarle Street.'

Nip, who had by no means enjoyed his stay in a house where he was confined to one room except for brief walks round the streets when his mistress felt she simply must allow him some freedom, saw the door open and darted through it, yapping on a high, infectious note so that

158

Sherida, chasing him and clipping on his leash, was moved to exclaim, 'We know how you feel Nip, but just be patient for one more little hour, and you will be in your own home once again!'

In fact, it was rather less than an hour later that they found themselves walking once more into the house in Albemarle Street and being welcomed by Bates, the butler, and Grieves, the footman.

'We've even missed the little dawg, sir,' Bates said confidentially. 'Cheerful little chap, Nip; kept us all busy, teaching 'im tricks and taking 'im for airings, when Miss was out.'

'Well, Miss Winyard will be happy to hand him over to you now, for I want a word with her, in my study,' the master of the house said irascibly. 'Not a moment to myself but I was being cosseted or pummelled or fed, but now we will talk about your allowance, if you please, Miss Winyard!'

Sherida, following his broad back meekly into his study, intercepted a glance between the butler and the footman which made her writhe. It was one of the knowing looks so frequently exchanged between old retainers when they think themselves to be participating in a lovers' tiff, or something of that nature. *And Grieves can be no more than twenty-five,* she thought irrationally. *What right have either of them to assume that Lord McNaughton and I are anything to each other?*

They entered the study, and Lord McNaughton motioned Sherida to a chair and took the one opposite. 'Now, Miss Winyard! About my . . . accident. It was no accident, save that you were the intended victim, we are both agreed on that score, are we not?'

She nodded, her expression intent.

'And the solution is to discover who is making these attempts on your life, so that we may take definite action against him or her. Is that right?'

'I suppose so.'

'Well, I do see that the whole thing would be clearer if I could but speak to your lawyers, but how to do it without leaving you, which is more than I dare do? You are in my care, but an expedition to Norwich would be a major undertaking, what with a chaperon for you and a nurse for me!'

'But why is it necessary for either of us to see Mr Jobson? What could he do?'

'He could tell us, my dear child, on whom the estate would devolve in the event of your death.'

'I see,' Sherida said. 'If I were to marry, of course, the estate would go to my husband, but if I were to die unmarried . . .'

'Precisely. If you could marry at once, and secretly, so that no one got wind of it until after the ceremony, all would be well, I'm sure, but you're still a minor, and in any case as your guardian I could not countenance such a havey-cavey business. Tell me, Sherida, whom do *you* suspect of nearly braining me with that jardinière?'

'My Aunt Bertha told me that she had taken Aunt Caroline up to see the floral decorations on the balcony, at Aunt Caroline's request. And she mentioned that she left Aunt Caroline up there, tidying herself and bathing her brow with cologne, for she had the headache.'

He nodded, frowning. 'But it could have been almost anyone, of course, even Diane or Roland! You don't know who inherits after your death?'

'I've been racking my brain to think,' she confessed, 'but the truth is, I've no notion! It never occurred to me, you see, that I might die a spinster!'

He smiled at her ingenuous statement, but said with a great deal of understanding, 'My dear, I should hope it did not occur to you! And even so, the person trying to do you harm may be doing so in ignorance of the true circumstances which would occur if you were to die unmarried. I think our best plan is to bait a trap!'

'With me acting as bait, I suppose? Charming!'

'I think it would be best,' he went on, disregarding her remark, 'if we put it about that I'd gone down to Norwich to consult with your Mr Jobson. In fact, I shan't leave London. I've a friend in lodgings in Dover Street, hard by here, and I shall stay with him so I can keep an eye on your comings and goings. You must send me a message as soon as anyone asks you out. Cora is reliable, is she not? Then she may be our messenger.'

'But what about Aunt Fanny?'

'It would never do to tell my mother. She

would upset all in her wild efforts to see that neither of us came to harm! You and she must carry on just as usual, as though nothing in the world had occurred to upset you, in fact. You have plenty of invitations; take them up!'

'There's a masquerade at the Billings', Almack's, and then Aunt Fanny has a card party at the Jerseys' and I am promised to Lord Lothbury. He is making up a party to go first to the theatre and then out to supper somewhere. I suppose an attempt might be made at any of those functions?'

He regarded her frowningly for a moment. 'You could be right, but I don't think so. The last attempt was too nearly disastrous for the murderer to risk blundering again. After all, someone might have spotted the guilty party sneaking down the stairs after the attempt, but not recognising it *for* an attempt, would naturally say nothing.'

She nodded. 'Yes, I understand you, I think. If something of a similar nature occurred again, questions might be asked. Very well, what is our next move?'

'Why, to inform all our acquaintances that I shall be away for several days; I shall make a point of telling both your aunts and cousins that I am to see Jobson. I think this will seriously worry someone, and another attempt will be made; this time, we shall be ready! Are you willing to come with me now, to the Tilneys and the Winyards, or do you have other plans for the rest of the morning?'

'But we've only just arrived home from the Winyards, won't it seem strange to go back there so soon?'

He smiled. 'Yes, it will; all the more reason, perhaps, for our return! I *want* your aunts and cousins to worry about my going into Norfolk!'

In the event, their visits were paid after luncheon, for Lady McNaughton showed such distress that Greville, who had been in bed for three days, might go out in his phaeton or even the barouche without a meal inside him, that they judged it wisest to assure her ladyship that they were in no hurry, and delayed their departure accordingly.

Sherida, glad of the opportunity to change her morning-dress for something more becoming, joined his lordship outside the front door, crisp and cool in green and white tafetta, her face framed by a chip-straw bonnet which tied under her left ear in a froth of green silk ribbons.

'Neat as a pin, Miss Winyard, and complete to a shade,' his lordship said approvingly. 'We'll go first to the Winyards, I think.'

They arrived at the Winyards house to find the family assembled in the hall, about to go off to the Botanical Gardens in the barouche, but they professed delight to see Lord McNaughton so soon, and ushered them into the library to discuss which of the balls, routs and assemblies they might meet at, during the course of the next few days.

'Naturally, we refused all invitations while your lordship was ill in our house,' Aunt Bertha explained. 'But now that you are better, we thought we ought to socialise once more, for dear Dolly's sake. After all, the child is only here for a few weeks before returning to Norfolk to prepare for the wedding, so I feel she should make the most of her stay in London.'

'Oh, that reminds me, have you any commissions for Lord McNaughton, Aunt? He is going down to Norwich tomorrow for a few days,' Sherida said innocently. Her aunt, looking a little surprised, said that that would be scarcely necessary, since they had barely returned from Norfolk themselves above a week.

'What are you doing down there, McNaughton?' Sir Frederick enquired jovially. 'Can't make head nor tail of Sherida's agent's report, I'll warrant!'

'No, I probably shan't be visiting Knighton,' Lord McNaughton replied easily. 'I want to see Jobson about one or two things. His office is on Castle Meadow, I understand. A strange name for a street!'

'Aye, that's right. You can't miss the street, for it is opposite the castle itself, which stands high above the city. Well, I wish you joy of the journey, my lord, for it's a powerful long pull.'

After that, conversation turned to other subjects, and they left shortly, since they had other calls to make.

The Tilneys were in, and Roland and Diane welcomed them heartily and were full of solicitude for Lord McNaughton's injury, though Sherida thought her aunt a little abstracted and quieter than usual. She avoided her niece's eyes, but almost every time Sherida glanced towards her, her eyes were fixed on Lord McNaughton with a thoughtful expression in their depths.

'Aunt Caroline couldn't take her eyes off you,' she announced gleefully as they set off homewards once more. 'When you told her you were going to Norwich, what did she say? I was asking Diane about their masquerade; they are uncertain whether to hold it after all. But they want us to join them for another evening at Vauxhall. It seems there is a famous soprano singing there. I begin to think it *must* be my aunt!'

She was only half-laughing, but he grinned at her. 'When I mentioned I was going to see Jobson she gave me a hard look and said "very wise!" I begin to think it *cannot* be she! But we must see who falls into our trap.'

'As long as it isn't me,' Sherida said. 'Be sure you don't let this trap go wrong Lord McNaughton, so that I'm victim as well as bait!'

He looked at her seriously, the smile quite banished, an expression in his eyes which drove all thoughts of murder out of Sherida's head and made her heart hammer in her breast. But all he said was, 'I'll see you safe,' and then, lightly, 'And when all this anxiety is over, I shall take you to a public masquerade, a very vulgar and shocking thing to do! One goes masked and disguised, of course, and enjoys the romp without taking too active a part in it. And after that, Astley's will be open. You'll enjoy *that!* The equestriennes are unequalled, and the spectacles amazing.'

'Well, that heartens me for the ordeal ahead,' Sherida returned lightly. 'When do you leave for Norwich, sir?'

'Tomorrow. Nothing much transpired this morning in the way of invitations — Vauxhall was too vague, no date was mentioned, was it, but I am sure something will crop up once I am thought to be out of the way. You won't forget to let me know your every movement? Promise?'

'Considering it's my life which depends upon it, I think you may safely assume I'll not forget,' Sherida said with mock indignation. 'And now we'd best talk about something else, for we are turning into Albemarle Street, and if your mamma knew about this . . .'

'It would never do, would it? Even a whisper of such perfidy would have her locking you in your room and making dreadful accusations to your relatives, I'm sure of it!'

'And since I am to bait the trap, *that* would never do,' Sherida concluded.

The carriage drew to a halt and he helped her down on to the flagway. 'My poor child! Would you prefer it if I took Mamma into our confidence and confined you to the house with an imaginary epidemic cold for a few days whilst I went to Norwich in all truth, to see what I could discover? Only I fear it might not stop the attempts on your life.'

He stood facing her, his hands on hers, a quizzical brow lifted. Sherida, flushing, shook her head decidedly. 'Goodness no, I am not such a coward as to think *that* would solve your problem! I am very sure that this torment will only be ended by catching someone in the act of trying to . . . well, kill me.'

He nodded, and led the way into the house but in the hall, turned back to her abruptly. 'Miss Winyard! Keep Nip by you!'

'I will.'

She proceeded to climb the stairs towards the drawing room where, by now, Lady McNaughton should be, having completed her shopping, but as she reached the head of the flight she glanced back. He was still standing with one hand on the study door, but he was looking up at her. The angle at which the light fell on him threw the scar into prominence, giving him once more that cynical, brooding look which she had not seen on his face for many weeks. Then he had turned and was gone, leaving her staring down into the empty hall.

CHAPTER NINE

'Is Lord McNaughton back from Norfolk yet, cousin?'

Sherida, now a veteran of the waltz, completed her twirl before assuring Roland composedly that he was not; scarcely could be, in fact, since it would take him the best part of two days to reach the city, and two days to complete the return journey.

'He cannot drive himself, for his shoulder is still bandaged,' she explained as they walked off the floor to join the family party. 'But the jolting and swaying of a stage-coach is not good for mending a broken bone either, so he will be driven down quietly by Lady McNaughton's coachman in the big travelling coach, and will break the journey at Newmarket, or Royston. But I daresay he'll be back by the end of the week. Why, Roland?'

They were at Almack's with Bertram and Dolly, Diane and Mr Unwin, and Aunts Caroline and Bertha, and Sherida noted with approval that the aunts seemed to be getting on much better and had, at that moment, their heads together over the best place to buy a really fashionable bonnet.

Continuing their conversation as he pulled up a chair for his partner, Roland said, 'Because of our expedition to Vauxhall, cousin! If Lord

McNaughton is still away, then it would be pleasant for you to come with Diane, myself, and Unwin. And we thought Mamma might be accompanied by Sir Edward Daventry, an old friend. Quite a little party, you see! How about tomorrow night?'

The elder ladies, having settled on the Pantheon Bazaar as quite the cheapest place for bonnet trimmings, turned their attention to the discussion.

'Tomorrow night is the Jerseys' card party,' Lacy Tilney said reproachfully. 'I *had* hoped to attend that, Roland dear!'

'And so you shall, Aunt Caroline,' Sherida said at once, 'for I am promised to Lord Lothbury. He is taking a party to see Edmund Kean, at Drury Lane! I am greatly looking forward to it.'

'Well, upon the following evening then? Have you any engagement?'

Sherida smiled up at Roland, trying to forget that this might be the trap. 'Nothing that I cannot break, cousin! But should I invite Lady McNaughton, or is this to be a family party once more?'

He hesitated, but said punctiliously, 'Certainly, if she wishes to come! But I had thought . . . that is . . .'

'Well, I am fairly sure that she already has engagements for that evening,' Sherida said, taking pity on his confusion. 'Thank you very much, Roland, I shall be happy to join your party,' she added, dimpling at him.

Aunt Caroline said comfortably, 'Very prettily said, niece! And tell Lady McNaughton I shall take the greatest care of you, and see that you are chaperoned! Not that she need worry, I'm sure.'

Soon after this the ladies went off to play cards, and presently Roland took Sherida's arm and they went into the supper-room. Already sitting at a table, talking earnestly, were Mr Unwin and Diane, and Sherida said, 'Mr Unwin seems to be getting very particular in his attentions to Diane, does he not, Roland? Is he a good sort of young man? He seemed very pleasant, that evening at Vauxhall.'

'I think he's on the point of making a declaration,' Roland admitted. 'I am glad if that is so, for Diane is fond of him and he's an old friend of mine. And though one should not set store by such things perhaps, he is heir to a good property, in Sussex. I believe he will speak to Di before he says anything to me, but he's made his feelings clear already, in his own way.' He paused, gazing down at her with his soulful eyes. 'How nice it would be, coz, if Diane and I might announce our engagements at the same time!'

She could not escape his meaning, but she replied as lightly as she could, 'I didn't know you were about to become engaged, Roland, but then I don't know you terribly well yet, do I? Who's the lucky young lady?'

'You little devil!' he said appreciatively. 'Why do you think I plot and contrive to get you to

170

myself for five minutes? Meet me in the park to-morrow, before breakfast, and I'll whisper the name in your ear!'

'Early? You'd not much like *that,* for Diane has told me how fond you are of your bed!'

He protested that he had managed to wake early enough on the previous occasion when he had met her in the park, and that for another assignation of a similar nature he would rise earlier still, at dawn if necessary, but she only laughed and he did not pursue the subject.

'So it is settled then?' he asked her as he saw her to her front door later that night. 'I will call for you here, and we shall go to Vauxhall and hear the new singer, whose voice is said to rival Catalini. And then we will dance, and walk, and eat supper in the booth.'

'I shall look forward to it,' Sherida said politely, though with doubtful sincerity, and went indoors to compose a note for Lord McNaughton.

What does one wear to foil a murder attempt in? Sherida asked herself with mordant humour, eyeing her gowns just before she was to dress for her evening at Vauxhall. Lady McNaughton, looking very fetching in rose-coloured silk, with a wrap of palest pink and silver taffeta, had left some time before with her escort, to join a party of friends who were visiting the opera. She had said gaily, as she popped in to bid her ward enjoy her evening, 'The weather is so delightful, my love, that you could wear your flimsiest gown with impunity.'

But if one wore one's prettiest gown to reject a proposal in, was it not being unkind to wear something so encouraging? And Sherida was fairly certain that whatever else might happen that evening, Roland would make her an offer.

Discretion might urge her to wear a dark shade, but her own optimistic nature won, partly because the dark colours in her wardrobe were few. Instead, in a defiant mood, she chose a narrow white satin slip edged with a ruffle of lace and worn with an overdress of lemon-coloured gauze. White satin slippers, pearls, and three yellow rosebuds in her hair completed her toilet. Cora, smiling at her mistress's appearance, adjusted the rosebuds in the knot of hair on the crown of Sherida's head, gave one last touch to the glossy ringlets depending from it, and stood back to admire her handiwork.

'Many a beauty has bemoaned that yeller is a cruel colour to be fashionable in,' she remarked to Sherida's reflection in the mirror. 'Blondes say it makes their hair look dull or dark, girls with dark complexions say it makes 'em look darker, and those young ladies blessed with a high colour say it turns roses into peonies. But you, Miss, if I might say so, can wear it to the manner born.'

'Yes, I do you credit,' Sherida acknowledged with a mischievous smile at the maid's somewhat dour expression. 'Thank you, dear Cora!

And now I'd best go downstairs to await Sir Roland; I don't want him to keep his horses standing on my account!'

She had barely arrived downstairs, however, before Roland was at the door, and bowing over her hand.

'You look good enough to eat, Sherida,' he declared, taking her hand and ushering her out to the waiting coach. 'Mamma and Diane are already in the carriage, and Mr Unwin and Sir Edward will meet us inside Vauxhall itself.'

They climbed into the coach, and Diane and Aunt Caroline greeted her with enthusiasm, both determined to enjoy their evening. But Sherida knew that for her, the outing would be marred by the miseries of suspicion, and by her necessarily furtive attempts to see whether Lord McNaughton had managed to find her in the crowd.

For crowded it certainly was. Within a few moments of entering the gardens and meeting Sir Edward and Mr Unwin, she realised that so far as murder attempts went, it would be very difficult indeed to find one's target amidst the shifting multi-coloured throng of fashionables.

In the pavilion, seated on a small hard chair and listening with only half her attention to the young, full-bosomed Italian who was singing her heart out on the stage, Sherida tried to glance casually at the audience. But it was impossible to see more than a fraction of those surrounding her, and in the end, she gave up the attempt and tried to concentrate on the music.

After the concert, she, Diane and Mr Unwin and Roland strolled in the grounds, whilst the older couple repaired straight to the supper box. 'Everyone is here tonight,' Roland informed her, 'just to hear that young woman. Look, coz, there's the Duke of York!' Sherida stared at the small, fat man with the red face, moving easily amongst the throng. 'He has a great *air* about him,' she commented at length. 'But he isn't princely, or anything of that nature, is he?'

Roland agreed that he was not princely, and then pointed out other famous people to her, keeping her amused with gentle, slightly malicious gossip about one or the other until they rejoined Lady Tilney and Sir Edward in the supper booth and sat down to their own meal.

It was whilst she was tucking into roast chicken and salad that Sherida saw Lord McNaughton — and such was her surprise that she very nearly choked. He strolled past the booth, a dark figure just outside the circle of light, but unmistakable to Sherida. He was dressed conventionally enough in blue coat, pantaloons and hessians, but when he turned a little towards her, she gasped so that a piece of chicken went down the wrong way, making her cough. For his countenance was ornamented — and obscured — by a great growth of whiskers, black and fiercely sprouting, so that, but for his walk and the well-remembered lines of his powerful figure, she must have believed herself mistaken.

No one else seemed to notice the unusually hirsute stranger, and shortly afterwards Roland begged her to walk a little way with him, and she rose gladly to her feet, hoping she might see his lordship again.

'Miss Winyard, your wrap,' the waiter called, and came after her, the lemon silk scarf over his arm. She thanked him, but it was scarcely necessary, so warm and pleasant was the night. She said as much to Roland, who had been glancing a trifle discontentedly at the people milling about on the path.

'Yes, it's very mild,' he agreed. 'Would you like to stroll along the dark wall, where there are no lanterns? It is very romantic.'

'No, thank you,' Sherida said briskly, shaking his arm slightly. 'But I would like to walk over to the lake you can just glimpse between the trees! Diane says there are beautiful red and gold fish in the waters.'

So it was beside the lake, with other couples about, and a cluster of thickly growing scented shrubs close at her back, that Roland proposed.

Sherida, fully aware that her life might well depend upon her reply, one way or the other, was a little more circumspect that she would normally have been; there was no point in courting disaster.

'I told you the other day that I didn't know you very well, Roland, and you don't know me very well, either. The truth is, I'm not going to give marriage a thought until the Season is nearing its end, and perhaps not even then! I am only seventeen, which is young to have a come-out, and I've led a very sheltered life. I might so easily mistake affection for love, which would be dreadful, wouldn't it?'

'You advise me to hope, then?' Roland said, in a throbbing tone calculated, Sherida thought, to impress her with his sincerity. Actually, it set her teeth on edge!

'Well, I like you very much,' she said soothingly. 'Please, Roland, don't press me, for I very much wish to remain friends with you and Diane, though I cannot promise any warmer feelings towards you, or indeed towards anyone else, at this time.'

'I have sometimes thought you might have some degree of warmer feeling for Lord McNaughton,' Roland said with some hesitation. 'He is, of course, a much better match than I, for I have little to offer beside my love, and my property in Kent which you've never so much as set eyes on. Though that, of course, can be remedied! I don't know if he's spoken to you on the subject, but . . .'

'No, he has not,' Sherida said hastily, hoping that the darkness would mask the tide of colour which rushed to her cheeks at the mention of Lord McNaughton's name. Heavens, but he might be hiding in the clump of bushes at her back at this very moment, listening with cynical amusement to every word! So she said firmly, 'I don't wish to marry *anyone*, Roland, but I *do* wish to return to your mamma now, please.'

Later, they danced on the stage which had been cleared for the purpose, and Diane and Mr Unwin were plainly seen holding hands both on and off the dance-floor.

'I can see a declaration will be made soon,' Roland managed to whisper to Sherida as he handed her in to the carriage at the end of the evening's entertainment. 'I will drive you home first, and then Diane and I will take Unwin to his lodgings. Mamma, of course, will be taken home by her beau!'

'Why did we have to leave so early?' Diane pouted, as the carriage moved off. 'I love fireworks, and the excitement.'

'Because I've been warned it might get rowdy here later,' Roland answered. 'There is a cockpit nearby which has been holding what you might call a gala night of their own — some big championship, I gather — and when they finish, a lot of drunken ruffians lurch into the gardens. And women of an unsavoury sort follow the men, and things may get out of hand.'

So, somewhat to her relief, Sherida found herself deposited on her doorstep before midnight for once, and felt she had brushed through her first proposal very well, all things considered. She also felt the heady relief of one who had expected to encounter danger and has not done so — with a little flatness, it must be confessed, that all her fears had been for nought.

When the knocker sounded she was halfway

up the stairs and she turned and looked towards the door which Bates was opening, half hoping that it might be Lord McNaughton, come to talk over the non-events of the evening with her.

It was not his lordship. A lad with a note in his hand stood there, murmured something briefly to the butler, the note changed hands, and the lad disappeared into the darkness.

Bates, turning from the door, said, 'Miss! I thought you'd gone up by now, but this note is for you. There's candles lit and the fire in the small salon, if you would care to read it in there.'

'It won't take a minute,' Sherida said, taking the note from his hand. It would be from Lord McNaughton she was sure. But the light in the hall was dim so she stepped into the small salon and spread out the single sheet. A glance was sufficient to tell her that the note was not, however from his lordship. Her eyes flickered to the signature. Bertram! What was he doing writing notes to her at this time of night? She began to read.

Coz, I do not know where to turn, I am being blackmailed by an opera dancer. She has a foolish letter of mine and will sell it back for twenty pounds or jewels to that value. She is to meet me at one o'clock in Vauxhall Gardens, by No. 8 supper booth. I know you go to Vauxhall tonight with Roland and if you could slip to the supper booths at one o'clock, with the money or, perhaps, your pearl drop earrings, I could have the letter back. You know how short Mamma keeps me, and I dare not tell her why I want the money. Do come, coz! I will wait for you by the booth at one o'clock, pray don't fail me,

Bertram.

Two thoughts flashed into her startled mind. First that the note had been held up and should have been delivered before she left for the Gardens, and then she could have confided some of the story to Roland and ensured that they were still in the Gardens at the appointed hour. Or, better still, she could have despatched either the money or her pearl earrings straight to Bertram. As it was, only by going to the Gardens herself could she now make sure that Bertram got his letter back and retained his good name.

The second thought was more sobering. The note might have been deliberately delayed to lure her, alone, back to the Gardens. Her cousinly fondness for Bertram would not allow her to let him down in such a predicament.

She glanced more closely at the paper. Was it Bertram's hand? Impossible to say, for in fact she had never received a written communication from her cousin in her life though she had seen his signature scrawled on the title page of books, or a few lines of writing in an exercise book. It is certainly like, she thought doubtfully. But the most amateur forger could make writing similar, and it did sound rather like the sort of scrape a boy like Bertram might easily fall into. The thought that Bertram might be her enemy she considered only for a minute, then shrugged it off. Ridiculous! She could not be relied upon to destroy the note, and if harm did come to her in the Gardens, he would be the first suspect!

What should she do for the best? But she knew. If it was true, then she must go to her cousin's rescue; if it was a trick to lure her to the gardens then she must appear to step into the trap. She would send Cora, with the note and an explanation of her own actions, straight round to Lord McNaughton's lodgings and then he could follow to see that no harm came to her. If it was no more than the truth, then she and Bertram would pay off his opera dancer with Sherida's pearl earrings and his lordship could remain in the background.

But suppose Lord McNaughton was not yet back from Vauxhall himself? He might easily not have realised her party were leaving and might have lingered, believing the attempt would be made when the fireworks began.

Bates, outside the door, gave a small cough. Abruptly, Sherida made up her mind. She would go but she would take Grieves, the young footman, with her. No one would expect her to go through the streets of London at this hour without a male escort.

Accordingly, she joined Bates in the hall and explained that she had to return to Vauxhall. 'Would you send Cora to me? And Grieves? I would like his escort. And would you summon a hackney?'

Cora arrived and stood waiting whilst Sherida dashed off a note to Lord McNaughton, taking great care to make her position clear. She would go to the gardens by river; after that, she was in his hands.

As she gave the note, together with Bertram's epistle, to the maid, Grieves came in to announce that the hackney carriage awaited Miss; she squeezed Cora's fingers. 'My dependance is upon you, Cora,' she said in a low voice. 'Put this into his lordship's own hands and make sure he reads it before you leave the house.'

Cora, privy to the fact that someone was trying to harm Miss, said fervently, 'I won't fail you; he shall have the note even if I have to hammer the door down.' Smitten by an inspiration, she added, 'If you was to take me up in the hackney, Miss, just as far as the end of the road, you might see for yourself that it was put into the master's hands and no other.'

So the three of them climbed into the hackney and Cora was put down at the corner of Dover Street and Sherida strained her eyes until she saw the front door open and Cora step inside, raising one hand in a gesture to show that her mission was as good as accomplished. Then they drove on, towards the Thames.

Once on the river bank, Sherida was insensibly cheered to see that the Gardens were, apparently, as brightly lit and crowded as ever. The little boats were busy, but she soon realised that most of the gentlefolk were coming from an evening of pleasure and that the type of person now embarking to go to the gardens was far from genteel.

However, this failed to suppress her good spirits. In a few moments, perhaps, she would know who was trying to kill her and would be free of the miserable uncertainty which had characterized her attitude ever since Lord McNaughton's accident. That she might, in the event of a mistake, be dead, she refused even to consider.

They found a boatman free to take them across, though not without difficulty, for though the crowd was good humoured enough, they were pushful and eager to cross. However, Grieves proved equally determined, and seizing her arm with a muttered, 'Excuse the liberty, Miss, but we'll never get over, else,' he proceeded to shove and elbow, saying whenever any remonstrated, 'The lady's got to get back to the gardens urgent; excuse us!' which seemed to work like a charm, for they soon found themselves in a boat and heading across the water.

Sherida kept her eyes fixed on the shore they had just left and presently thought she made out a familiar figure, holding one arm a little stiffly as he climbed into a boat. Smiling, she turned her gaze towards the gardens. She would be safe now, and might give herself up to the enjoyment of entrapping her enemy.

Soon enough, she and Grieves were at the entrance, Grieves was obtaining their tickets of admission, and then, for the second time that night, she was in Vauxhall Pleasure Gardens.

CHAPTER TEN

Inside it was even more crowded than Sherida had feared, but only around the big central stage, where the dancing had become a wild romp and the figures cavorting to the music were not by any means well-bred. But further on, where the crowd had thinned, she could see that the paths and grottoes must be almost deserted, and she rather thought the supper booths would be in darkness. It was very late, too late for any further meals to be served.

She and Grieves began to push their way through the crowd, but as she neared the outskirts of the audience who watched the dancers a man, far gone in drink by the look and smell of him, caught her by the arm. 'Little Miss Sary, by all that's wonderful,' he bellowed. 'Little Lady Sary, come to dance wi' old Reuben Prosser!'

She saw Grieves, unconscious that she was not following him, forge purposefully ahead, then lost him in the crowd. She tried to pull away and her silk scarf fell to the ground. She watched helplessly as it was carried from her by the scuffling feet, then Mr Prosser was bellowing, 'Lady Sary's lost 'er shawl! Come on, fellers, 'oo took Lady Sary's shawl?'

He struggled after the scarf, which was now being passed from hand to hand ahead of them, towing the reluctant Sherida behind him.

Raging helplessly at her position, she tried to look around for Grieves, but there was no sign of him. Deciding tact and humour were her only weapons, Sherida said gaily, 'Thank you, Mr Prosser, but that . . . er . . . shawl belonged to an old aunt of mine whom I never could abide. I'm glad to see it gone, and want none of it. Good evening!'

For a miracle, he took the remark at face value. 'Lady Sary don't wan' that pretty shawl,' he said mournfully. 'She don' wannit acos she's got an aunt . . . By God, Lady Sary, I'm your fren', for I've an aunt or two meself, an' miserable ole trollops they be! I 'member onct . . .'

He had let go of Sherida's arm in order to gesture more freely and she was able to move away from him, wriggling with quiet determination through the crowd until she reached its perimeter. She would have liked to search for Grieves, but behind her, a lament made itself heard. 'Oy! Laaady Saaary! Where's she gone, the luv? I gorrer shawl I 'ave, me bucko! Where's she gone?'

A dark, bold-eyed woman was looking at her fine clothing and pearls with unmistakable greed, and Sherida's heart sank. She could not linger here, with the woman staring and the voice of Mr Prosser growing louder!

Turning her back on the crowd, she began to walk resolutely towards the supper booths. She saw they were in darkness, save for one or two at the extreme end of the row which were, presumably, still being tidied up. Most of the lanterns had been doused but here and there a faint, coloured star twinkled in the trees, and in any case, she had no choice. She must go on, to the eighth supper booth, and if Bertram did not appear then she must lurk nearby until either Grieves or Lord McNaughton came searching for her.

She drew level with and passed half-a-dozen booths but on approaching the seventh, a feeling began to prickle the back of her scalp, telling her that someone was watching, unseen. The feeling was so strong, so compelling, that almost instinctively she swerved off the main gravel path and down a narrow, winding way between dark trees and shrubs. As she did so, she glanced back at the eighth supper booth. Running out from its shelter was a dark figure, unidentifiable in the faint starlight, but wrapped around in a hooded cloak which Bertram, she was sure, would not have been seen dead in. The figure could have been man or woman, and it entered the pathway even as she whisked herself round to run with all her might in the opposite direction. She glanced back once, and saw the gleam of a blade held low against the dark cloak.

She reached the end of the narrow way and burst onto a broad, gravelled walk, bounded by trees and flower beds. She scarcely paused to consider which direction to take; she was running all out now, holding up her narrow skirt and wishing desperately that she had chosen a less conspicuous shade. White and yellow must stand out beautifully, even in the darkness under the trees. Her feet skidded on the gravel as she realised with horror that this path was no escape route — it led straight to the little lake where, earlier, she and Roland had watched the fishes while Roland proposed to her.

Again, instinct saved her from a check. Without consciously re-living the events earlier in the evening, she swerved into a narrow, unfrequented path which would lead, eventually, back to the supper booths. And the path was thickly lined with rhododendron bushes. Halfway up the path she risked a quick glance over her shoulder. Her pursuer was not yet in sight. Without a second's hesitation, Sherida flung herself flat on the ground and wriggled beneath the sheltering branches of a large rhododendron.

Seconds later, the cloaked figure came into view. Trotting steadily, the knife gleaming, breath coming in quick, uneven rasps. Sherida peered, but could make out no features in the white blur of the face.

Then the figure stopped. Almost like an animal, it seemed to be scenting the air. Slowly it turned and Sherida knew, with a feeling of most uncanny terror, that her pursuer had divined in some mysterious way that she was not ahead, but hiding.

Fear froze her immobile and she scarcely breathed whilst the dark hollows in the white blur swung slowly round, probing the bushes for a glimpse of white and yellow, ears pricked for the slightest rustle, nose atwitch for the faintest breath of perfume, almost scenting the air for her fear.

Then the figure moved forward again. At a jogtrot it rounded the corner. And from ahead, Sherida heard the crackle and rustle of someone pushing their way into the bushes. So the hunter was not deceived! By forcing a way into the shrubs her pursuer would be able to see anyone hiding against the lighter background of the sanded path!

Quick as thought, Sherida slid out of her retreat and began to run back up the path. She joined the main walk and risked another backward glance. Her pursuer was coming round the corner! Breathless now but winged by fear, she ran on. If only she could have a minute to think what best to do! She wanted urgently to run towards the stage and the warm, convivial crowd, but she had lost all sense of direction. She plunged into another side path, then another, running almost blindly, her mind intent on one thing only — escape.

And then, after she had dodged and run and run again, disaster struck. She entered a long, straight avenue, planted with trees, swerved up to the left and ran hard up the straight. At the end, a flight of steps led up to a small temple, thickly surrounded by bushes. In the moonlight, for the moon had risen, the place looked ethereally beautiful, but she could scarcely see for the sweat which stung her eyes, could scarcely hear above the thundering of her heart. All she could do was run, driven on by the fear of the knife.

Her pursuer was flagging, she could tell that. But the distance between them seemed to get no longer. The other's breathing was horribly noisy now, the footsteps seeming to blur and slide more. But Sherida was tiring too, and she did not have the knife. She reached the steps of the temple and glanced wildly to either side. It would be perfectly possible to dodge into the bushes, but not to escape. They were so thick that she would be caught in them, like a fly in a web. Up the steps she ran, into the temple, then turned like a wild creature at bay to confront her pursuer, who was just beginning to toil up the steps.

At that moment, the figure raised its head and looked up at her. The hood of the cloak fell back, revealing the face drained of colour by the moonlight, the lips drawn back over bared teeth, the eyes narrowed with a fanatical gleam.

Aunt Bertha!' Sherida breathed. 'Oh, Aunt Bertha!'

Aunt Bertha gave no sign that she had heard. Half-crouching, she was climbing the steps, her eyes fixed on Sherida's face with no recognition in their depths, only a sort of mindless blood-lust which terrified Sherida more than the steadily held blade.

Where, oh where, was Lord McNaughton? Why had he not appeared to seize her aunt long since? But he had not, and it seemed as though she must act now, or it would be too late.

'Aunt Bertha!' Her voice was thin, but strong enough. 'Aunt, it is I, Sherida! Why do you point that knife at me? Put it down!'

Aunt Bertha's heavy, rasping breath was held for a moment as though she considered, and then she laughed and Sherida saw foam fleck her lips. 'It's for my baby, my darling,' she said in a crooning mutter. 'How can I tell my son that Knighton will never be his, just for a scruple? When with one little thrust of this blade I can give it to him!'

'But he's marrying a rich woman, Aunt,' Sherida said, trying to keep her voice steady. 'Why should he want Knighton?'

'Dolly Ainsworth? Rich? She's not even in line for her father's property! It's entailed upon a distant cousin! It was only when he declared he loved Dolly that I knew you must die. Before, I thought if I frightened you a little, that would keep you from courting young men other than Bertram. Once I knew he intended to marry a penniless little nobody, I had no alternative. You have to die, so that Bertram can have Knighton. His father may fail him, but I shall not!'

'So it was you, Aunt, who threw the dog into my mare's path, and shot at me while I watched the fireworks? But why, Aunt? Why did you not ask me for Knighton?'

Aunt Bertha gave a sly, hoarse giggle and fingered the knife, slowly advancing a step nearer

190

her niece. Sherida stood firm and saw two figures rise from the bushes, exchange a signal, and begin to creep up the steps. She felt quite weak with relief as she recognised Lord McNaughton, his face strained and white, his eyes fixed steadily on her aunt's back. But Aunt Bertha was mad; who could say what might happen if her rescuers pounced?

'Aunt Bertha, I have friends climbing the steps behind you. Put the knife down and turn round slowly. Don't be afraid.'

Another evil-sounding snicker of laughter answered her, then her aunt sprang forward, the whites of her eyes showing, her teeth bared in a horrific snarl.

Sherida staggered back with the madwoman's breath hot on her face, saw the knife suddenly twist in the air and fall, harmlessly, at her feet, and then Aunt Bertha lay beside it, motionless, and Lord McNaughton's arm was round her in a tight hug, his voice was saying comfortingly, 'You're safe, my child, quite safe!' He turned and spoke to his companion. 'Bertram, see to your mother.'

Sherida saw that the second figure was indeed her cousin Bertram, and that Grieves was just emerging from the bushes and mounting the steps towards them. Bertram dropped to his knees beside his mother. He moved her, tried to lift her, then lifted a pathetically white face to theirs.

'She's . . . she's dead,' he said, his voice

breaking on a sob. 'I can feel no heartbeat.'

Sherida detached herself from his lordship's embrace and knelt beside her cousin. She picked up her aunt's limp wrist, but no comforting pulsebeat moved beneath her fingers. Lord McNaughton, kneeling beside her, said heavily, 'She's dead. I imagine she had a heart attack. I'm sorry, Bertram, but perhaps it's for the best. She could not have been happy, confined.'

'She did it for me,' Bertram said, unashamedly wiping tears from his eyes. 'Ah, God, how could she have thought I'd want Knighton on such terms? I've got all I want — the home farm, and Dolly.' He got to his feet. 'I'll take her home now. What shall I tell people, McNaughton?'

'Just that she had a heart attack, I think,' his lordship said. He raised a brow at Sherida. 'Will that suffice, my child?'

'It's the truth. You'd best take charge of the knife, sir.'

She handed him the blade and he took it without comment and slipped it into his pocket.

Grieves, who had stood a little back from them now came forward. 'Beg pardon, sir,' he said respectfully, 'but if the lady had a heart attack, there won't be no questions asked. The excitement of an evening at Vauxhall is well known and has resulted in an attack before, what with the fireworks and all.'

Bertram, with his mother's body in his arms, said brusquely, 'Now that's settled, I take it we can leave,' and strode out of the temple and down the steps. His mother's face, against his dark sleeve, looked peaceful, with no shadow of that leering, maniacal expression which had so terrified Sherida.

At the gate they found a sympathetic boatman who rowed the party and the 'sick lady' across speedily and then found them a carriage.

'Go with Mr Bertram, Grieves,' Lord McNaughton told the footman. 'And as soon as you arrive at the house, summon a doctor.'

They saw the sad little group off and then Lord McNaughton tucked Sherida's hand into the crook of his arm and led her to where his coachman was walking the horses, patiently awaiting his master's return.

'I'd only just returned home when your message came, so I sent to the stables and Jacobs brought the carriage straight round. Jump in, child, and I'll see you home to Albemarle Street. In fact I shall come home myself, and explain my presence by saying I found it unnecessary to go to Norfolk after all.'

In the coach, Sherida said dazedly, 'It was Aunt Bertha who fired at me, you know, that first time at Vauxhall. Why did she lead me to think it might be Aunt Caroline?'

'She did not, you dreamed that up all by yourself. She did, however, try to convince us both that your Aunt Caroline was responsible for my accident.'

'And what of Bertram? How did he come to be with you, this evening?'

'Bertram's no fool. He knew his mother had arranged the jardinières herself, at her party, had actually met her coming downstairs after the pot had been pushed off the balcony. But he said he'd not have suspected anything if Lady Winyard had not been at such pains to convince everyone that Lady Tilney had been upstairs at the time of the accident. He knew she hadn't, you see. She and Diane were waiting in a downstairs room for their escort to take them to the opera. Lady Winyard knew nothing of that, of course. And the more Bertram watched his mamma, the more worried he grew. He had heard his mother once bemoaning the fact that if you married, the estate would never become their property, and Uncle Frederick rated her sharply, it seems, for covetousness.'

'I see. But that doesn't explain Bertram's presence at Vauxhall tonight.'

'He saw his mother leaving the house wrapped in a dark cloak, and followed her. He dropped behind though, and arrived at the river bank, where I was about to embark, after she had disappeared into the crowd in the Gardens. I showed him the note you'd received and he went ashen, poor fellow. He agreed to accompany me, but insisted that though she might play a foolish trick upon you, she would never do you harm. That was why I waited, before giving the signal to climb the steps. I wanted him to hear from her own lips that she had murder in her heart.'

'Poor Bertram,' Sherida said softly. 'How terrible, to realise one's mother is mad.'

'And bad. There was no charity in her, to plot such a thing in cold blood. But let's talk of something pleasanter.'

'Yes, indeed. What a dreadful evening this has been. I feel as though nothing nice will ever happen again!'

He smiled at her and moved across the carriage, to sit beside her. Slowly, his good arm went round her shoulders and he pulled her to him, saying breathlessly, 'Oh, my own darling!' as he began to kiss her. He felt a slight initial resistance and then she was warm and yielding against him, her lips soft beneath his, her heart beating like a fluttering bird against his own breast.

Presently he said into her hair, 'I've longed to do that — oh, for weeks past! But it was too damned dangerous. I kept suggesting marriage, but you never rose to the bait, and to court you in form was more than I dared do!'

She lay in the circle of his arm, but at this she twisted her head to look up at him, and pinched his hand. 'Suggested marriage? With everyone but yourself as bridegroom, you mean! And you were so horrid when I got into foolish scrapes! And . . . and you've thought me like my mother, haven't you?'

He caught her to him again, kissing her with a fierceness which roused an answering fierceness in her own breast, so that she wound her arms round his neck, murmuring endearments against his demanding lips.

'You're a darling,' he said at last, when they drew apart again. 'I didn't want to fall in love with you, but having done so, I know you're the only woman in the world for me. I love you and intend to marry you, Sherida Winyard!'

'And I love you, Greville McNaughton,' Sherida said. 'Though you were abominably rude to me, and so cross, and the family said it wasn't me you wanted, but Knighton! I certainly didn't want to fall in love with you! Uncharitable people will say *he* married *her* for her property, and *she* married *him* for his expectations!'

'Do you care?' The coach was drawing to a halt and he kissed her again.

'I care only for you. And now you'll be more conceited than ever!'

'Very true.' Lord McNaughton climbed down frown the carriage and held out his good arm, swinging her easily and tenderly to the ground. They climbed the front steps and he let himself in and held the door for her. She glanced round once before going into the hall. The sky was lightening with dawn, and a faint flush of rose on the horizon heralded a new morning.

Standing in the hall, where the candles were still lit in expectation of Sherida's return, though all the staff had long gone to their beds, he pulled her towards him again, his expression softened with love. 'One person beside ourselves will be very glad,' he said softly, just before their lips met. 'My dear Mamma has

196

always longed for a daughter.'

The kiss was prolonging itself until Sherida felt they had almost fused into one ecstatic whole when a voice said accusingly, 'Greville! What *are* you doing, kissing Sherida in the hall at this time of night? I declare, your manners get worse and worse. Let the poor child go to bed and kiss her again in the morning, after you've both had some sleep!'

They moved apart quickly, both eyeing Lady McNaughton with mingled surprise and guilt.

She came down the stairs, smiling fondly at them, her pink silk dressing-gown with its ruffles of lace looking almost like a ball dress. 'Foolish, foolish children! What has brought this on at such an unseasonable hour? I could have told you you'd make a match of it from the first moment Sherida stepped into this house! *Made* for each other, I told Cora, *weeks* ago! Now upstairs with you; we'll send the notice to the *Gazette* in the morning!'